PENGUIN BOOKS

GW01066331

Sofia Taylor

PENGUIN BOOKS

PENGUIN BOOKS

Published by the Penguin Group
Penguin Books Ltd, 80 Strand, London WC2R ORL, England
Penguin Group (USA) Inc., 375 Hudson Street, New York, New York 10014, USA
Penguin Ireland, 25 St Stephen's Green, Dublin 2, Ireland
(a division of Penguin Books Ltd)
Penguin Group (Australia), 250 Camberwell Road,
Camberwell, Victoria 3124, Australia (a division of Pearson Australia Group Pty Ltd)
Penguin Group (Canada), 90 Eglinton Avenue East, Suite 700, Toronto, Ontario, Canada M4P 2Y3
(a division of Pearson Penguin Canada Inc.)
Penguin Books India Pvt Ltd, 11 Community Centre,
Panchsheel Park, New Delhi – 110 017, India
Penguin Group (NZ), 67 Apollo Drive, Rosedale, North Shore 0632, New Zealand
(a division of Pearson New Zealand Ltd)
Penguin Books (South Africa) (Pty) Ltd, 24 Sturdee Avenue,
Rosebank, Johannesburg 2196, South Africa
Penguin Books Ltd, Registered Offices: 80 Strand, London WC2R ORL, England

www.penguin.com

First published 2008
1

Written by Georgina Newbery
Based on the series *Sofia's Diary*,
created by Nuno Bernardo and written by
Marta Gomes, Melanie Martinez, Danny Stack

Copyright © Beactive, Produções Interactivas, S.A. 2008
All rights reserved

The moral right of the author has been asserted

Set in 10.5/15.5pt Sabon
Typeset by Palimpsest Book Production Limited, Grangemouth, Stirlingshire
Printed in Great Britain by Clays Ltd, St Ives plc

Except in the United States of America, this book is sold subject to the condition that it shall not, by
way of trade or otherwise, be lent, re-sold, hired out, or otherwise circulated without the publisher's
prior consent in any form of binding or cover other than that in which it is published and without a
similar condition including this condition being imposed on the subsequent purchaser

British Library Cataloguing in Publication Data
A CIP catalogue record for this book is available from the British Library

ISBN: 978-0-141-32670-2

www.greenpenguin.co.uk

Penguin Books is committed to a sustainable future
for our business, our readers and our planet.
The book in your hands is made from paper
certified by the Forest Stewardship Council.

Contents

March   1

April   31

May   73

June   117

March

15 March

Hey, I'm Sofia and I'm writing on a clean, clear, empty page in a book Jo gave me as a leaving present. She's cute, that girl. She knows me. The paper's sort of satiny and super-smooth white. And I've got a pen that gliiiiii-iiiiiiiiiiiiiiiiiiiiiiides over the page. It's nice. Feels nice. See?

So, I'm here in my new room in my dad's house wondering how I got here. When I say 'room', I mean recent ex-dumping-ground attic. Though it's definitely got potential. There are windows between the sloping roofs and a bed big enough to float away on in my dreams.

I texted Jo to tell her I landed safely but haven't heard back yet. Jo's my best friend . . . or was. How long does a best friend stay that way when you live hundreds of miles apart? Stockport and London aren't exactly next door to each other!

I've been sent to live with my dad. And his new wife. And their two-year-old little boy.

Because I'm un-livable with at home.

That's what my mum thinks.

My mum's not speaking to me. Hasn't spoken – apart from instructions and information – since . . . Oh, I'm still too angry to talk about it, so I'll save it and tell the story later when I'm calmer!

Anyway, here for your reading pleasure, is a little bit about me. I like:

1. Music – all kinds so long as it speaks to me somehow, on some kind of level. I like music when it makes my hair stand on end. I like it when it makes me moooooooooooooooooooooove. I like it when it makes my heart sing high in the sky with the birds and the clouds and the sunshine.

2. I like my friends. A lot. I need my friends. I mean, I'm seventeen years old. These are the relationships that define me. My family are a given, I didn't choose them (who would?!) but my friends are people I choose to be with me.

3. I like being unique, individual, unmistakably Sofia Taylor. And to do that I have to make my own style. So I customize my clothes. Quite often I make things from scratch. Oh yes, I can wield a sewing machine, I know how to thread a bobbin. Listen, I don't mind a bit of arcane equipment if it means I don't have to worry about looking the same as anyone else. I hate the idea of walking in somewhere and finding I'm in the same bland beige-and-lilac outfit decreed THE look for spring.

So I like mad hair and fishnets over vicious pink tights. I like long hair because you can be a stern miss one day and the Lady of Shalott the next. I like to paint my nails all the colours of the rainbow and wear odd earrings. I've got a great spidery non-pair: one's lots of strings of oily black beads, the other lots of strings of mother of pearly pink. I put my hair up high off my face and go for a matt, powdered look and some serious eye make-up. It's great. I'm seventeen. I'm allowed to experiment. One of these days I'm frightened I'll wake up like my stepmother and never wear a colour again!

16 March

So how did I get to be here in a freshly cleared out attic in my dad's house?

Because my mum found drugs in my room at home.

Did I say they were mine?!

The whole situation's outrageous.

1. What was my mum doing going through my drawers in my private room?
2. How can I make her understand it wasn't me who put those pills there?
3. How little does my mum know me? That's the worst bit. There's no such thing as innocent until proven guilty, at least not in my family. No matter how many times I say those pills weren't mine, I feel like I've been tried and convicted and am now behind bars in one of those stripy jumpsuits.

Living here's going to be tough. Dad and I . . . put it this way, I haven't spent a birthday with him since he and my mum split. He has a new wife, Emma (my Stepmother/Model/Actress/WHATEVER!).

SMAW has this young yet bossy thing going on the style front. Kind of not very hip outfits, sort of trying to be cool, with this mummy/teacher's pet look: long girly hair and cream sweaters with just a tiny bit of glitter in a naffly tied scarf. And somehow she's got my dad in a matching sort of cream cotton crew-neck vibe – sooooo freebie catalogue couple! Cream. Cream and beige. Cream, beige and grey. I'm inventing a new colour to describe them – GREIGE! This house is crying out for some ORANGE!

And they've had a baby (the Devil Child). I haven't had a conversation yet with Dad, or SMAW, which hasn't circled somehow around Devil Child and back. He's barely two years old! He's the baby and the only boy. Guess how popular he is? Well, I tell you what, I'm going to wear flowers in my hair and pink satin slippers and jangle bangles around him so he has some light and music in his life!

Dad looks at me like he's a rabbit caught in the head-lights – I wonder what Mum told him? My mum and dad divorced years ago. I stayed in Stockport with her, until she married my stepdad, and he and Trisha moved in. Trisha's his daughter. And we kind of managed to co-exist – till last term . . .

OK, so how would you react to the following scenario? You walk into a classroom to find your boyfriend kissing your stepsister. You'd go ballistic, right? I blew up the chemistry lab. It was meant to be a trick to blame on my now EX-boyfriend, John, but it backfired and somehow the entire chemistry lab went up in flames. I didn't mean to do it, honestly, but I got suspended.

Is London paved with gold? If I could see the pavement for the people I'd tell you.

17 March

So, day one at college. It *would* be St Patrick's Day! What do you wear to your first day at a place where not a single person has ever heard of you and, therefore, your first impressions are fundamental to your future?

After a certain amount of style agony – like trying on my entire wardrobe in every different combination possible – I decided it's college, not a fashion show, and they can take me as I am. In the end I went for a kind of dark but studious look: skirt, not jeans, short but not too short; black tights; black suede waistcoat I got at a vintage shop in Stockport; and my faithful cream crocheted beret – sounds grim, the beret, but it feels comforting and my hair looks nice coming out from it and I like the way I can wear it every which way and be different people depending on the angle. I'm going to need ALL my different personas to make a success of myself at this new place!

'Good luck' text from Jo. 'Good luck good luck good luck good luck.' That's all she can send me from Stockport while she goes back to the beloved old same old: how I WISH I was her!

I hate this new-girl feeling! It's like drowning – only

you're surrounded by people who could save you, if only they even noticed you were there.

So, nobody notices my existence until I can't open my locker. Then they just stand around sniggering until I do. Great, now I'm the entertainment.

Then I managed to crash, literally crash, into little miss popular (apparently her name's Rebecca) and made her spill her papers all over the floor. No new friend for me there then.

One girl, called Jill, gave me a flyer for a party. She seemed all right. But she was giving flyers to everyone so she wasn't particularly inviting me. I didn't have the nerve to start up with something like, 'Hey, I'm Sofia. Would you like to be my first new friend?'

So I reckon I won't go to the party. I won't know anyone.

I know, I won't get to know anyone if I don't stick my neck out. But I hate being the one who has to risk their neck! It's not that I'm shy . . . Or maybe it is? Maybe I just never knew because I've been surrounded by the same people for years and years and years. Now I know what it feels like, I wish I'd been nicer to that girl who was new in my class last September. I thought she was snooty. Now I know she was probably just terrified!

How do I do this? Do I dance down the school corridors doing the cancan so that they all know I'm there? Do I give out flyers myself, advertising myself as a friend? It could read, 'Sofia Taylor: everything you've ever wanted in a friend. From loyalty to fashion advice, cool taste in music and strict aversion to football. Only poets and dreamboats need apply.'

I am being a bit mousy-mousy . . . but . . . will you stick with my moaning till I get the feel of school a bit, and maybe summon some confidence from somewhere, and eventually do the neck-sticking-out business and actively make a friend of my own?

I mean, it wasn't ALL bad . . .

There was one guy . . . dark, cool, aloof . . . black hair, black T-shirt, black leather jacket, black jeans. He just grabbed my hand, wrote an address on it and said there'd be another party on Thursday, same night as the flyer party. No goody-goodies, he said. And I redeemed myself by cooling it back and saying, one eyebrow cocked, that I might think of going. He's called Ray. Maybe I will go . . . I'm really not into the idea of a boyfriend right now . . . but nobody said there was any harm in just flirting!

18 March

Day two of college, imagine this: I'm there, keeping quiet, trying to fade into the non-existent wallpaper. I even wore this goofy bobble hat I got in my Christmas stocking with flaps that cover my ears: it comes right down over my eyes when I want it to – great hiding gear. Anyway, at the end of English the teacher thinks he's my new best friend and starts running this whole 'say no to drugs' campaign on me. Even though I have zero interest in taking any! The man actually gave me a 'Talk to Frank' leaflet. I didn't expect the floor to swallow me up but it would have been nice.

On the same subject (feeling sorry for me) let me just get a few things about Dad and SMAW off my chest:

1. Aren't they a bit old to behave like love's young dream all the time?
2. I haven't moved to London exclusively to provide un-paid childcare for Dylan.
3. Dylan = Devil Child. It's not his fault, I know he doesn't mean to but go within a three-metre radius of him and you won't get away without being smeared with half-chewed biscuits – or worse!
4. And the poor child's never left alone for a minute: either it's googoo googoo eat, or googoo googoo sleep, or googoo googoo fly in the air. He should make the most of the attention: it won't last.

SMAW . . . I know she doesn't want me there. A seventeen-year-old stepdaughter's not exactly what she needs to complete her picture of happy families.

For a start, I must make my dad look older to her friends. And to her. Remind her how he's way past forty. Which she should be able to tell by the way he dresses like a sort of middle-aged version of something from Topman in an effort to make himself look young. But there she is all smiley and friendly, encouraging me to go to the party advertised on the 'trendy-looking flyer'.

Trendy!?!?!

And then I get another head-on-one-side, being-nice-to-me, 'how are you settling in?' chat. A little lecture about how going to parties can be a good way to meet people.

I know they must be trying to help but, honestly, when was the last time they walked into a room of people they didn't know and had to go through the agony of waiting, and not looking desperate, for anyone except the nearest dork to come up and say something to them?

So, two different party invitations but no friends.

19 March

Am I the only seventeen-year-old in the whole world who'd do anything *not* to go to a party?

SMAW and Dad are on about it all the time. It's a vehicle for all the points they want to make to me:

1. Good for you to get out there.
2. But be careful to stay away from drugs, Sofia.
3. Special dad voice that goes with the one about 'keeping it down' while Devil Child goes to sleep, saying something about 'the choices you make now go towards turning you into the person you're going to become later'.

What he's saying is that he doesn't want me to be the kind of girl who goes round getting off her head and blowing up the school. Well, just for one final time, THEY WEREN'T MINE AND I DIDN'T! It was the chemistry lab and it was an accident. Will anyone EVER believe me? Aaaaaaaaaaaggggggggggggggggghhhhhhhhhhhhhh!

College no better. Ray (cool aloof one who wrote on my hand) almost stopped to say something but little miss popular (er, why?), Rebecca, accidentally on purpose bumped into me just as I was finishing a text to Jo and made me drop my phone – which she then kicked halfway down the corridor. So Ray walked off leaving me to the mercies of Jill (leaflet distributor) who brought it back.

Actually, a guy called Sean handed it back. Jill introduced him. He seems all right. Bit goofy. Sort of jiggles up and down all the time as if he's not sure what to do with his great big long arms and legs. Jill doesn't give much away. I mean, she looks cool enough. But that's it. She *is* cool. Not warm and welcoming. Except she IS speaking to me, which has to be a start.

Sean said if I went to the flyer party I'd know them to talk to. Jill's brother's DJ'ing. Doesn't sound goody-goody to me – sounds cool. What's Ray's party got to offer – other than Ray? But I'm not sure about Jill, looks like she doesn't want me to come and rain on her parade. I STILL DON'T KNOW!!!!!!!

Look at me! Two parties to go to and no friends! If Jo were here, see, then we'd get all dressed up and take both parties by storm. When Jo's around it doesn't matter what else happens – I've got a dancing partner, someone to escape to the loo with, someone to giggle behind my hand with when there's a gorgeous guy to blush at . . .

I mean, these guys, Jill and Sean, I bet they're fine. They might be my new best friends. It's the MAKING of the new best friend bit that's such a trauma. So much work. So much smiling and standing about, hopefully shifting from foot to foot . . . and then, to be really good mates they've got to tell you ALL about themselves, and you ditto, and that takes more than a 'How ya doin?' at a party. See what I mean?

20 March

Dad's decided I have to pay for the damages at my old school – which weren't my fault, in case you haven't got that yet – with work experience at the completely un-wicked *Wicked* magazine.

It's just like they say: fashion people take what they do sooooo seriously. You'd think from the way they storm about all desperate about a seriously random celebrity's new fringe that there's no starvation, no war, no crises anywhere but backstage at some designer's show.

I'm there to dogsbody. My desk is right beside the photocopier and features nothing more exciting than a great big flashing phone. My boss is Alice. Super tall, and thin as the grande skinny sugar-free vanilla lattes she likes. Specially sugar-free – she's a real sourpuss with a face like a cat's bottom and no sense of irony at all. The skinny sugar-free blah blah latte she orders is given exactly the same level of importance as the photo shoots she organizes. I'm in charge of the lattes – some responsibility!

Still, I have to say it wasn't all bad. This guy slid out of the lift at the end of the day and said 'Hey'. Put it this way, I wouldn't say no if he offered to buy me a . . . what would I have? Iced-fruit smoothie: raspberry, orange and pineapple.

And the really good thing about this place? It's heaving with design stuff. At least in THAT area I'll be in my element. My homework's going to be so over-designed that hopefully the teachers won't notice if the content's a bit slapdash.

And then, home again, and old SMAW turns up in the doorway to my room, all sweetness and light, and hands me the most horrible top you can ever imagine and says she thinks I don't want to go to the party cos I've got nothing to wear!

I mean, I guess she meant well but, seriously, it was so bad that if it was the last piece of clothing in existence I'd go naked till the end of the world. And then Dad came and joined in, both of them standing in the doorway, heads on one side, all 'Go on, go to the party'.

Why don't they go and try putting themselves 'out there' as they call it?

Well, if they're so desperate then I will go. I found some old clothes in a cupboard, customized them, and *voilà*! Not so bad. At least I don't look like I've got no imagination at all. And nobody'll be wearing the same as me.

Pre-party friend count – possibilities:

1. Ray, cool to look at – not giving much away, though.
2. Jill, she might be cool but she's not exactly welcoming me with open arms.
3. Sean, bit of a Labrador puppy. Cute? Maybe.
4. Josh at work. Gorgeous eyelashes.

Which one do YOU like the sound of?

So here goes. I'll tell you how it all went later.

21 March

In the morning. I'm leaving in the morning.

I don't give a toss who's friendly. I don't give a toss for all the effort I've made to settle in and go to parties and make friends.

I'M GETTING OUT OF HERE SOOOOOOOOOO-OOOOOOO FAST!!!!!!!

Will Jo's mum let me stay? I doubt *mine* will.

What a mistake I made going to that guy Ray's party! Everyone was out of it and being sick. Ray offered me a pill . . . it would have been so easy . . . but I didn't. All I wanted to do was get out of there.

I don't know. Do you have to do all that stuff to be cool? He IS cool. At school, at least. He's a kind of lounging loner. The sort who reads poetry and makes it tough at the same time.

But between you and me, that kind of being-sick-in-corners, out-of-control sort of party – it frightens me. It's all so . . . rank! Does that make me square as a pair of regulation school shoes? It's just . . . maybe I'm just a stupid romantic but I'm into walks in the park, kicking piles of autumn leaves in the air, listening to music by the light of the late-afternoon sun. Getting drunk and taking pills and being sick in corners is just not me.

Big girl, grown-up girl, good girl . . . I wish!

Anyway, I told Ray I had to go and meet my friend, Jo – IF ONLY! And I walked off down the road in the dark, and I found a random bus stop and stood there in the dark for I don't know how long, hoping the bus I needed to get to the other party would come.

It's weird, London. You think everyone's going to try to do you over one way or another, when in fact all they do is aggressively ignore you – I wouldn't dare ask a stranger if I was going the right way. I was – but that was completely by chance in the end.

And the party Jill gave me the flyer to? I got off the bus where the driver said I should and there was just this big wide road and barely any street lights and nothing. Except the muffled thud of a music beat. What could I do but follow the sound? Search out the sound? And, eventually, down this alley . . . there was the gleam of light round the edge of a door, and a couple of people coming out and the sound and the light splashed all over the place and I was so relieved to have found the place I nearly grinned at these people!

It was a cool party. I loved the music. Jill's brother's a great DJ. I kind of shuffled about for a dance with Sean, just because he asked me – he's cute, kind of goofy. So in the end not such a bad night. I got myself around

London without getting myself killed, and got myself home – an adventure in itself for a Stockport girl like me.

But THEN . . .!!!! I walked in to a load of verbal from SMAW and Dad. Like, completely out of the blue. They'd been sitting up waiting for me. I bet they painted those black rings under their eyes with her eye shadow just to make more of a point – it wasn't even two o'clock and it's a BANK HOLIDAY tomorrow. Anybody ever heard of a lie-in?

She'd scrubbed herself up into a right lather. 'Parently that heap of old clothes I thought were for the charity shop were SMAW's best designer labels.

WHAT??? Well, I wouldn't have cut them up if I'd KNOWN, would I? If she had any taste they'd LOOK like designer clothes. It's a stupid top I customized not the Turin Shroud. So I'm going. Tomorrow. Getting out of here at last . . .

22 March

I went to bed in my clothes and stared hard at the ceiling all night, waiting for dawn to come tapping on my sky-high window. Then I threw the essentials into my old mirrored bag and headed off before anybody was up. Even Devil Child still slept as I tiptoed past his room, carrying my trainers. Outside it was a cool wet London morning. The pavements smelt metallic from the rain in the night. The city seemed empty. Nothing but rubbish skittered along the pavements. I took the 68 all the way to Euston. There were daffodils out all over Camberwell Green. And new leaves on the plane trees flapped like see-through acid yellow/green taffeta in the grey light.

Jo texted to say it's snowing in Stockport.

I texted back, 'I'm coming home'.

London's kind of beautiful when there's nobody in it. When the bus went over the river you could see the Houses of Parliament and the Eye and all sorts, and the river itself was this great flat satin ribbon. There are all these immense cream-and-grey buildings along the river and very few boats. And there was nobody else but me and the bus driver and the occasional person getting on and off.

It was strangely lovely. Calm. I felt like the city was all mine.

Until I got to Euston and the woman at the ticket box said a single to Stockport today would cost me a hundred and twenty quid!!!!!!!!!!!!! In my rush to escape I hadn't thought about money.

I went and sat in a coffee shop and drank a cappuccino very slowly. I read a discarded copy of yesterday's *Standard* minutely from one end to the other. I knew what I was going to have to do but for that hour I didn't acknowledge anything but that I was enjoying my solitude. When nobody knows who you are, and it's not the middle of the night, it's OK to be on your own.

And then I got back on the bus and it wound its way all the way back to south London, heading into watery sunlight the whole way. I let myself into the house and I could hear Dylan giggling in Dad and SMAW's bed. The door was closed. I tiptoed upstairs and back to my room. I guess they'll never even know I was gone.

I'm stuck here now. For the indefinite . . .

I've got to find the strength to make the best of it from somewhere.

When I got up to my room I got some shots and reminders of Stockport I had brought with me and started making a kind of collage for my wall. I need a good printer. And a good scanner. But for the moment I'll have to make do.

Do you find if you're doing something creative you can lose yourself in it and the troubles of your life fade away for the time you're concentrating hard like that?

24 March

Hey, Happy Easter. Maybe I've eaten too much chocolate but I'm having this thought that maybe my dad is kind of cool. Maybe, just a little. Or maybe just today. Or maybe I've fallen under the spell of Dylan aka Devil Child aka The Easter Bunny, who is actually JUST FOR TODAY kind of cute. OK, I've definitely had too much chocolate.

My mum always does this thing (which my dad calls 'melodramatic' whenever he talks about it), where in the middle of a really heated argument she just suddenly stops speaking. It's like the sound is cut and the whole world freezes for a moment, like the woman has superpowers. And it occurred to me on Thursday, after the whole Issey Miyake incident with Dad and SMAW, that I AM JUST LIKE MY MUM!! We both have a terrible temper, and we both have a tendency to think we can run from our problems. As my hero Bruce Lee once said, 'A quick temper will make a fool of you soon enough.'

Dad pointed out this little temper of mine on Saturday when we had a long talk without SMAW and he was surprisingly smart. He knew I didn't mean to ruin SMAW's clothes – but he hoped I would at least say sorry. He also pointed out, quite wisely, that running doesn't solve anything. You just leave a big dust cloud in your wake.

If I am going to do this (and by THIS I mean stay in London and give this new life a real try), the first thing I need to do – now that I have APOLOGIZED to SMAW – is stop running. This is Dad's idea, and I find it hard to admit he might be right. To quote my man Bruce again, 'To hell with circumstances; I create opportunities.' Let's see what turns up here in London Town . . .

25 March

Bad day/good day? You decide.

So I'm flattered, if surprised, when little miss popular Rebecca says she wants to interview me on college radio. Seems I'm to be introduced to the whole place in one go. But, hey, maybe that's the best way to get it over with? Until I walked in there and the first question from Miss Squeaky Clean was 'Virgin or slut?'

WHAT???

She must have got into the school filing system or something to find out about Trisha coming on to John when he was MY boyfriend. How could she do that? How could the filing system have information about my PRIVATE life? The whole thing was bang out of order!

I pulled my mike off, and tried to get out but she wouldn't stop harping on. How else could I shut her up? I had no choice but to thump her.

I know! You don't go round thumping anybody. Doesn't help. Doesn't work. And not necessarily the WISEST of moves. A catfight on the radio? Nice way to be introduced to the whole college.

But here's the good bit. Turns out Jill's decided I'm worth something. She heard what was going on, went and got Mr Caring Sharing English teacher and he pulled the plug on the whole thing.

Jill said she should have warned me in advance; she even apologized. She told me never to trust Rebecca goody two shoes *ever*, that under that sleek exterior lies the witch from hell. 'The staff all love her. We know better,' said Jill.

We.

I like her. She's cool. And the fact she wasn't all over me like a rash when we first met but has warmed up since she's seen me around a bit, seen what I'm like, makes me think that she might like me properly, for who I really am. So, hey, look at this . . .

NEW FRIEND COUNT: ONE!

26 March

Dilemmas, dilemmas.

You know how when you make a new friend, ONE new friend, it's cool to help her out, no? Turns out Jill writes a blog. Loads of people read it. She reviews stuff, and says what she thinks. I told her about *Wicked*. She thought it sounded great. I told her it would be if my main ambition in life was to be a champion coffee orderer. I should get a job waitressing next; I'd be really good at that. Seriously, I've got a pretty good memory for 'one tall skinny sugar-free vanilla latte, two grande mocha cappuccinos, a fat blueberry muffin, an almond croissant and a bottle of Luscombe organic lemonade'.

Anyway, there are always advance copies of singles lying around and I told her we had The Ting Tings' new single and maybe I could get it for her so she could review it on her blog. Nobody else has shown any interest in it. It's just gathering dust. At least if she reviewed it, people who are actually interested in the band might read about them since *Wicked* aren't featuring them.

So I put the CD in my bag.

And gorgeous Josh, the one who slipped out of the lift and said 'Hey' like he liked me, saw me do it and gave me a little chat about how I couldn't take CDs, embargoes and stuff.

It was soooooooooooooo embarrassing.

I mean, he's, like, nineteen? Maybe? And he's telling me off!

I went a really flattering colour purple and told him I know about embargoes.

I do! I did! I wasn't going to suggest Jill review it till AFTER the single came out. But what's the harm in her hearing it? Maybe headlining the fact she's GOING to review it on her blog? It was so embarrassing. He must have seen the colour I went even though I sat there smiling all cool and relaxed like it's the most normal thing in the world to be told off for doing illegal stuff by someone about five minutes older than you. Though I suppose he must be a bit older than that. He's there full-time.

He is cute. Really. Brown hair. I like his eyes. He's kind of lanky. Goes for a sort of indie look. He doesn't order me to get coffee all the time. Not really a basis for a great love story – but you never know . . .

But back to the dilemma.

I told Jill I'd get The Ting Tings' single for her. And now I can't. Unless I sneak it out to her. But rubbish though the job is, life at home would be a whole lot worse if I got fired. Dad is a freelance photographer who does quite a lot of shoots for the magazine, and it turns out they're doing him a favour letting me work there. If I get caught, it'll be bad for both of us.

So, a single friend to my name and I might be about to lose her already.

27 March

They don't want me here. They really don't. Especially SMAW.

'Shall we take Dylan to the city farm, just the three of us?' No, no, leave me out why don't you? What would I want with googoo-googooing over a sheep with Devil Child?

Still . . . Good News: Jill invited me to The Ting Tings'

gig on Thursday. She's got two tickets and she's asked ME to go with her! At Shepherd's Bush Empire. Now THAT'S COOL. She could have asked Sean . . .

I think there's some kind of unfinished business there. I think they used to be into each other. But now . . .? I've got to find out. If you know these things then when there are atmospherics around a group you can understand where they've come from. If you don't then you just assume the atmospherics are directed at you. Or rather, I assume they're caused by me.

Jill says Sean's into me. I don't see it. He talks like we're in LA all the time. He's kind of dorkish. Nice but sort of nerdy. She's always teasing him. I reckon she might still be into him. We'll see.

Besides, last time I had a boyfriend he went off with my stepsister. Which kind of put me off the idea of going out with anyone unless I'm really, really sure of them. I mean, I can LIKE people. Doesn't mean I'm going to DO anything about it. I can't tell Jill I don't want a boyfriend. She'll think I'm a proper weirdo. But it really hurt when I found John copping off with Trisha.

So, since Jill's a mate, and a mate is the one thing I need more than anything around here, I'm going to get her that Ting Tings' CD. What harm can it do? She's just a college girl with a blog. It's not like she wants to break the embargo on the front page of *NME* or something, is it?

Seriously. It's never EVER my fault. Life's complicated enough without making trouble for myself. Most of the time I feel like I'm just about keeping my head above water, specially now – moving to London, new college, work experience.

But trouble seems to find me, wherever I hide.

In the end I didn't give the CD to Jill. I know . . . I was going to . . . but . . . It's just my dad works at *Wicked* too. So we'd both get into serious trouble if ever . . . well, what if Jill lost the CD or something before the embargo was up? What if it got into the wrong hands? I mean, I KNOW how unlikely that is given we're just two south London schoolkids but . . . in the end I decided it wasn't worth the risk.

Also, I forgot. I took the collage I'm making for my bedroom wall into work and in between coffee runs I was mocking it up into something seriously cool. And at the end of the day I'd made this giant glossy print-out for my wall, and I rolled it up and put it in a tube and took it home and clean forgot The Ting Tings' CD. Which you might think makes me sound vague and forgetful. But I took that as a sign. I had SUBLIMINALLY decided NOT to give her the CD. And so I wouldn't.

But when I told her, Jill had a conniption fit.

How *could* I have given it to her? I'd have got into sooooo much trouble. I'd hoped she'd understand that. I thought she was my friend. Instead, she sticks her nose in the air and says she's going to The Ting Tings' gig with

Sean instead of me (told you they have history). 'Cos he's a mate and mates don't let you down.'

Right – as if it's my fault I can't give her the CD. So I'm not invited any more.

Or am I?

Cute Josh at work said he'd texted to ask me to The Ting Tings. Yes, you heard me. Who needs Jill when there's a cool lanky indie Josh with eyes like an azure sea fringed by lashes thick as palm fronds to hand?

Haven't got the text yet. It's stuck out there in the ether.

But should I go with him or what? What do you think?

He must be cool. He sees through the fact I'm nothing but a dogsbody for Alice-it's-the-end-of-the-world-if-I-don't-get-my-coffee-NOW!!!!!!!!!! and doesn't care that she treats me like a piece of dirt caught on the spiked heel of her Manolos. He stands by with an amused look on his face while she desperately lists the bizarre colour scheme she wants her photocopying done in. He doesn't feel sorry for me: he just agrees she's ridiculous. And invites me out. It's not that I want the start of a great big love story – I just don't want to be ignored!

You know what? I really like writing this diary. I seriously need the privacy. I mean blogs are cool and a great way to say stuff you want out there but what about the private stuff? It's really cool being able to say what I think without half the world being able to read it and judge.

So, privately, here's the scary friend count. Once again we're back to . . . ZERO!

I'm homesick. I want to go home. I don't want to have to think about fitting in all the time. I want the things I'm used to, the life I'm used to. I don't want to have to learn so much every single day of my life. I want to take the bus into Manchester with Jo, spend the afternoon trying on outfits we can't afford and avoiding the bossy shop manager who always starts, 'Are you going to buy that, or what . . .?' I want to know exactly where I'm going, what there is to do, how much it's going to cost, that I can get home easily to a house where they want me to be.

My mates at home were soooooooooo jealous of me coming down here. They thought it would be so cool. All the hot clothes, clubs and music a girl could want. Interesting work (as if!). A cool college. I'll admit it: those things crossed my mind too.

Instead, I've pissed off the one person I could have called a friend – who turned out to be someone I could only be friends with if I did something illegal to buy her friendship.

I couldn't face any of it this morning. The whole thing, college, work . . .

So I decided to wag it.

I took my Oyster card and thought I'd explore my new world. Well, a trip to London town from anywhere else would be called an education, wouldn't it?

And I'll tell you what I learned:

1. You need a specialist degree if you're going to understand the *A–Z*. Nobody has this degree apart from black-cab drivers, who aren't going to stop and give directions to someone like me who can't afford to pay them.
2. London is, like, seriously crowded – so crowded you get crashed into the whole time when you're just trying to find where you are on the map while you walk down the street.
3. And when you're not being crashed into you're waylaid by flyer flashers. They say nothing in life comes free; well, let me tell you, I could have had any number of allegedly free hair cuts and massages, lunch, even, if I'd gone off with some orange sari-ed, shaven-headed dancers, who hopped up and down Oxford Street with rings on their fingers and bells on their toes advertising spiritual enlightenment, free rice and dhal.

I found a vinyl shop off Carnaby Street and I kind of relaxed into it so I could flick through some sounds and let the music soothe my troubled soul, when who should I look up and see across the aisle? JILL!!!! I steeled myself, ready for her to turn her back on me.

But here's the good bit.

She smiled.

And apologized.

Said she was sorry she'd gone off at the deep end.

She'd had stuff going on that had made her crabby.

She'd had no right to try to make me do something illegal.

We went out for coffee . . .

Phew!

Friends count? Back up to ONE!!!!!!

Oh my . . .!!!!!!!!!!!!!!!!!!!!!!!!

I just went to get something to eat downstairs. Nobody around. SMAW's diary was lying about on the kitchen table, cool as you like. So I looked at it. Course I wouldn't normally do something like that but something drew me to it. Something forced me.

And I was so right to look!

'Thursday, lunch with Tom.'

Last week she met up with Tom.

And the week before that.

And he's pencilled in the week after next too!

Who the hell's Tom? How could she? And what do I tell my dad?

April

1 April

Another good day/bad day in the life of Sofia Taylor.

Bad bit. Evidently my dad's being made the proper April fool. We're all having dinner together, right? He's all schmaltzy with SMAW and says, 'It was fun at the city farm –' Sure it was wicked! You wouldn't have been able to bribe me to go along with three tickets to see The Metros! Well, maybe, for The Metros – 'and maybe we should all have lunch on Thursday together.' More happy families. And SMAW goes, 'Yeah.' Innocent as pie.

I stared good and hard at her. She has her lunch with Tom scheduled for that day. Suddenly, she goes kind of white, flushes, then stutters, 'No, I've got a manicure.' What? Then it's her turn to be all lovey-dovey. 'I need to keep my nails perfect for you, my darling.' And she kisses his hand! What? And he just takes it all, like the innocent he is. Poor lovelorn fool.

Good bit. Jill came over to help me choose something to wear to The Ting Tings. I kind of told her about Josh. Just a bit. Didn't admit I fancy him or anything.

It's cool to talk about boys. Just cool, that's all. And I hoped my telling her about Josh would get her to open up about the Jill and Sean story. I swear she still fancies him, whatever their history. She said they used to see each other. Like years ago. When it was more holding hands in the playground than serious romance. They were at primary school together. She can't remember a time she didn't know him. And now he's like her brother, she says. She reckons she quite fancies this guy Scratch, who plays with Sean and Mikey in their band. But she thinks he's got a girlfriend and so doesn't know what to do about that.

I told her I'd try to help her find out. I mean, there's no point making eyes at someone if they're occupied elsewhere, is there?

But Jill doesn't seem to mind too much which way it goes with Scratch. With her it's all family: her nan's fried chicken, her mum's big family dinners, her brother's DJ'ing. I think she needs to take some space for herself!

Besides, she says her last boyfriend turned out to be a real nasty piece of work. I told her I knew all about that! I told her about John and Trisha.

It's good, we know all about each other now.

I told her about Dad and SMAW and the mystery Tom too. She was as shocked as I am. I still don't know what to do. Course I don't want to admit I was snooping in SMAW's diary. But my dad has a right to know.

I tried to talk about it with Jo but it's tough being so far away from your true best friend. And she will always be that. Like best friends in the playground. Best friends forever.

What would you do? Tell your dad the love of his life's having an affair? Or go for the quiet life and keep shtum?

I can't.

I'm not the quiet sort.

He's my DAD!

2 April

It's sooooooooo embarrassing. Josh must know I thought he'd asked me on a date. You should have seen the shoes I wore to work! Silver glitter with heels to die for. Just the thing for un-jamming the photocopier in. Until I got the text.

Words to the effect of: Come to The Ting Tings and be my dogsbody.

Dogsbody! No, he didn't say that. More like: Come to The Ting Tings and help with my stuff.

But it's the same thing. THAT'S what he thinks of me. He likes me because I'm USEFUL? AAAAAAAAAAA-AAAAAGGGGGGGGGGGHHHHHHHHHHHHHH!

Anyway, I've said I'll go now, haven't I? He looked at my heels and said something like, 'Best to wear something sensible tomorrow night, Sofs.'

Like, sooooooooooooooo patronizing. He can really get up my nose sometimes. Perhaps I should make up something about having to babysit. But then I'd have to be in on my own all night while all three people I know in London are at a gig I'd DIE to go to. And now, to go, I have to crack open the old trainer bag just to make sure I look like some kind of roadie. Doesn't he want me cramping his style or something? Bet he's all skinny tie and stupid hat.

Trainers or no trainers, I might have to customize something to make a statement. After all, Sean and Jill will be there, and if they see me I want them to think I'm cool. They don't have to know that being the photographer's dogsbody's not a hot position I've been jostling for for weeks . . .

SMAW suggested we have a little chat today. You know . . . TALK about my problems and stuff. It took all my self-control not to throw something in her two-timing face. I still haven't had a chance to speak to Dad. The moment's got to be right. I can hardly just come out with it at breakfast in front of her, 'Hey, Dad, did you know SMAW's cheating on you?'

Can I?!

3 April

Tell? Don't tell?

Well, I did what I thought was right.

This is how it happened.

I saw SMAW kiss this famous Tom and cosy up to him in a restaurant this lunchtime. They weren't even hiding! They sat in the window and he stroked her hand, and she looked really upset, like she's working out how to tell my dad she's cheating on him. I had to tell Dad. It was, like, burning up inside me. He's my dad and she's cheating! It's not right.

I read somewhere that teenagers have seriously strong feelings of right and wrong – they called it the moral imperative. Well, I tell you, I felt a seriously strong moral imperative to tell my dad that SMAW was sitting holding hands with this other guy in a restaurant WINDOW for ALL THE WORLD TO SEE while Dad was out earning an honest crust to keep her and Dylan in this nice house and everything. It was OUTRAGEOUS!

But then . . .

I told him.

And he just went off the handle about me looking in her diary! Said I was out of order! And then he really turns the tables on me.

Seems like I'm not the only one with secrets.

Turns out this Tom is her mate from college who's a counsellor and they want me to go and see him! It's them who haven't been straight with me!

I told my dad that I'm not a loony, I'm fine. I'm no more screwed up than anyone would be who's had the following dumped on them for no reason at all:

1. My boyfriend's been stolen by my stepsister.
2. I've been blamed for being in possession of drugs that weren't mine.
3. I've been kicked out of home in Stockport.
4. And sent to live with strangers, in a strange town, halfway through my A levels.

I reckon I'm pretty sane, considering.

And now I have to go to The Ting Tings and play dogsbody to big boy Josh. Maybe I will go and see this counsellor. Maybe I'll fall in love with HIM – that'd teach SMAW and Dad to meddle.

4 April

So much for the great office romance. Not that I ever really thought it would come off.

But I kind of said . . . implied . . . to Jo.

Well, it's difficult. She's got a new boyfriend. She'll feel bad if she goes on about him all the time and I've got nobody to talk about. So . . . OK – OK! Honestly, I did secretly think that even if Josh only wanted me as his dogsbody at least he wanted me. But . . .

So we went to the gig, right? As I predicted he was in some really flash gear, and there was me in my stinky old trainers and jeans and an old Gap hoodie – practical but not exactly glamorous. He took pics for, like, ten minutes or so, and muggins here spent the entire gig weighed down with his lenses and different cameras and battery packs and all that. There was this pack of girls all over him like a rash and he just showed off like he was really important and kept dumping stuff on me. I mean, the music was good but the experience was pants!!!!!!!!!!!!!!!!!!

This was my first time at Shepherd's Bush Empire but, seriously, I hardly saw anything I was so slung about with luggage. And at the end – this was the most mortifying bit of all – at the end I thought, OK, so now we can enjoy ourselves, yeah? And Josh turns round, with all these girls hanging off him, and says like I'm his slave, 'You take the stuff home, Sofia Slavegirl.'

Well, those weren't his exact words but that's what he meant. And I heard myself stammer something about coming along to the after-party and he said, 'I don't think you'll get in where we're going wearing those trainers!!!!!!!!!!!!!!!!!!!!!!!!'

AAAAAAAAAAAAAAAAGGGGGGGGGGGGGGHHH-HHHHHHHHH!!!!!!!!!!!!

I WISH I'd worn my silver high heels, and I wish I'd just dumped all his kit on the floor in front of him and told him where to stuff it. I could see Sean and Jill. I could have gone and hung out with them.

But no – I actually picked up all those unbelievably heavy bags and dragged them halfway across London on a night bus! And THEN I took all this stuff of his into work and he was all matey matey. 'How ya doin', girl? Cool night, or what?'

Well, NO, actually. It wasn't very.

I saw Jill's blog. I saw the shots SHE took. And I saw Josh copping off with one of those girls hanging off him when he should have been working.

Office romance my – I'd no more have anything to do with someone like Josh Angelo than . . . than . . . than I'd take up going to see a counsellor once a week like SMAW wants me to do!

I tell you, he's for it. He's NOT my boss. He's barely older than I am. I hope one day soon he trips on a camera strap IN FRONT OF A LOT OF PEOPLE and does himself a really serious injury.

Oops! Ripped the page . . . Where's the Sellotape?

7 April

Half-term. Other people get a break. I get two weeks' full-time work at *Wicked*. How wicked is that? NOT!!!

For the record – in case anyone ever reads this and finds any of it confusing – I suppose I have to make things clear: I DON'T GET PAID FOR ANY OF THIS WORK EXPERIENCE!

Or, rather, the something less than the minimum wage I get for the hours I spend there – fetching coffees and making photocopies all the colours of the rainbow – is going into a bank account, and when there's enough in there (years from now?) it will be emptied to pay back the damage caused by my explosive moment in the chemistry lab back at my school in Stockport.

Capeesh?

But things could be worse. Although I have to work all the way through half-term, when I'd really just like to veg about and listen to Sean and Jill talk about music all day long, I have, at last, been given the tiniest little smidgen of responsibility. Alice, my cat's-bum-faced (it's not her fault, she's just so stressed all the time), sugar-free-vanilla-latte-mad boss has asked ME – yes, little tiny useless old me – to be in charge of a rail of clothes for a shoot she's organizing this week. I've got to guard it with my life! Well, I've taken a chance and left the rail at work and come home without it. But, seriously, what can happen while nobody's there? I'm not going to win any prizes but maybe, just maybe, at last she has seen I'm more than just a coffee-fetching, photocopying robot!

So – the list's looking better:

1. Friends? Sean and Jill – definitely. Josh? No way!
2. Work? Fashion assistant at *Wicked* (for one week only). At least it's something to put on the CV, don't you think?

Jill wants to be a lawyer with a social conscience when she finishes her studies. How can she know what she wants so clearly? She's got a career path all laid out: A levels, university, law degree . . . She's focused.

Me? My dad clearly thinks I'm best off starting at the bottom at a fashion magazine. I'm not stupid . . . it's just . . . there are so many things. It was easier when I was five and could say, 'I wanna be a ballet dancer.'

And now?

Photographer?

Music something?

Fashion designer . . .? Like I'm really going to get in to Central St Martins with a couple of customized Issey Miyake tops.

I'm doing psychology, media studies, English and French A levels. The idea being that is wide enough to leave my options open. The problem is I don't know. I don't have a drive to do anything in particular.

I mean, Jill knows. She likes music but she knows the law's her thing. Me? I'm not sure my social conscience is so developed that I want to do something so . . . meaningful. It's not just that either: she'll get seriously paid for being a lawyer. But how BORING!!!!!!!!!!!!!!!!!!!! I'll never tell her this. But law . . . Isn't it just fusty old people shuffling through dusty tomes and saying things like, 'If I may cite the case of *Dull v. Duller* of 1739 when the number of mangle-wurzels in dispute blah blah blah.' I'm reading *Bleak House*. It's not doing my opinion of the law any favours.

Sean's funny. He doesn't believe I don't support a football team. Can't imagine it's possible! He plays in a band with Jill's brother, Mikey. They ARE cool. He is cool – because he doesn't know he is. Know what I mean? He's dorky and funny and doesn't care what people think about him – but he's sharp and his music's great and he's really into the stuff he's into – he doesn't just lie about all day waiting for life to come to him. I'm not saying I want to MARRY the guy or anything. But maybe I should be careful not to become too matey either. Don't want to end up like Jill is with him – knowing him too well to go out with him. But then . . .

What is this? I thought I didn't WANT a boyfriend?

Having a boyfriend implies a lot of things:

1. That I've got over John being traitorous with treacherous Trisha.
2. That I dare risk my heart again.

And . . . the big one:

3. That I think I'm here in London for good!

Is there any relationship you can have in life where some-body doesn't want anything from you? Manipulation, emotional blackmail – call it what you like . . .

Incident number one: so I bump into my dad at the coffee shop. I'm weighed down with a list of orders as long as my arm and he nods and smiles and says he hears I'm doing well at *Wicked*. Nice. Little smile. Warm feeling. Can he help me? Sure. Then, wham – 'Please go and see the counsellor, Sofia.'

Get out of here, Dad! Do you really think I'm mad as toast? Don't try to soothe me into a false sense of secu-rity and once you've got me feeling all warm and cuddly try to sneak that one by me!

Incident number two – less subtle but same difference: back in the office I find Josh fiddling about with the rail of clothes I'm supposed to be defending with my life. Knowing him as I do, I feel a disaster in the offing. I pull out the Golddigga dress Josh was putting back on the rail and, guess what? It's burnt!!!!!!!!! Not just mildly singed either: there's a great big black burn in the middle of the dress. It even smells burnt.

'It got too close to the lights when I was photographing it.'

'You SPAM-HEAD!'

What was he doing photographing it? He wasn't supposed to touch it. He wasn't supposed to have anything to do with it!

We are in soooooooooooooooooooooooooooooooooooo

much trouble. Or rather, he is. That's what I said. And he said, 'No, WE!'

Like we're in this together – like, we're not.

But the horrible truth is that he's right. It's either him and me, or me and Alice the boss – and, as he says, if she finds out she's gonna fire me – no matter who else is involved. So I'm forced to lie and cheat WITH HORRIBLE JOSH because I have no choice.

I wish he wasn't so pretty – I know he reckons he can get away with anything because he's so good-looking. And it's true. He's probably spent his whole life getting breaks and stuff because he's cute to look at.

Well, Josh Nasty, here's something you've made me swear: I'm NEVER going out with anyone just because I fancy their looks. They've always got to have something more to them, something they've proved to me, before I'll go out with them. So nuurrrrrrrr!!!

9 April

More emotional blackmail. SMAW got a letter from school about when that witch Rebecca got nasty over the radio when she interviewed me. I can't believe they wrote a letter about it.

1. Isn't it all over?

And:

2. What is there to write a letter about?

44

Anyway, she said she wouldn't tell Dad about the letter IF I agreed to go and see the counsellor. They must think I'm really mad – or desperate.

What will the counsellor do? Brainwash me into being some perfect example of unreal teenagerdom? I mean . . .

1. I'm supposed to be difficult.
2. I'm supposed to be grappling with all sorts of issues.
3. My hormones are all over the place. I'm bound to suffer mood swings.
4. I'm NORMAL!

And, yeah, maybe things have been tough for me over the past few months, not mentioning any:

5. Two-timing boyfriends
6. Evil stepsisters
7. Moves to planet London
8. Changes of school
9. And making new friends . . .

. . . in particular. OK, so maybe the list IS quite long . . .

But that doesn't make me need anyone else to tell me how to cope with it all. I'm perfectly capable of doing that myself. Look, I'm up to date with my homework, I haven't wagged off school more than once, I do my horrible work experience – I've even managed to squeeze in making friends with Jill and Sean between babysitting duties and washing-up. I'm a walking miracle!

There is the SLIGHT problem of the burnt dress to resolve though. Alice nearly found it today . . . but Josh distracted her. I'm racking my brains for a solution and, so far, I've come up with zilch.

10 April

I don't understand. What makes people tick? What makes people work? What's OK and what's NOT OK? Lying? Cheating? For a DRESS!

So, Alice found out about the dress. Ballistic is an understatement. I don't see, I can't see, I'll NEVER see, what made THAT dress so much more brilliant for the shoot than any of the other twenty hanging on the rail.

Anyway, she gave me and Josh a BLANK CHEQUE (!!!!!!!!) and told us to just go and find another one, whatever the cost. She said it would come out of our salaries. At this rate, I'm going to be here forever, like an indentured servant, waiting and waiting till I've paid off my debts before I can look elsewhere for a LIFE of some sort!

So Josh and me took a taxi that waited with its engine running outside all the shops we went into, and we went round and round the houses looking for this stupid dress.

When we finally found it the girl in the shop said it was sold. So Josh batted his pretty eyelids and lied about how important he is, lied about how important *Wicked* is, promised her a mention, practically asked her out!!! He did persuade her that we'd pay her about four times what the dress was worth to have it and could she lie, a tiny little white lie, and get another one for the customer? The girl took the money. We're all crooks in this game. We took the taxi back to the studio.

Question: if I did all that lying and cheating and spending money like it's water in my personal life and got found out I'd get into SOOOOOOOOOOOOOO much trouble. But because it's work, it's OK. Really?

At least Josh said he'd pay the money back himself so I wouldn't have to. That doesn't exactly mean he's redeemed. But I'm speaking to him.

11 April

So that's it. My tiny weeny little bit of a love interest – OVER! He's such A DODO!!!!!!!!!!!!!

AAAAAAAAAAAAAAAGGGGGGGGGGGGHHH-HHHHH!!!!!

I'm all over the place. I'm so angry I could SPIT! How could Sean have let me down like this? I LIKED him! I thought he was funny, clever – CLEVER! Now he just turns out to be as gormless as any pretty boy with nothing better to do than fiddle with the product in his hair. He was cool! I liked him.

OK, so the bad news today came pretty thick and fast.

Bad news item ONE . . . Rebecca's got work experience at *Wicked*. Yes, she with her butter-wouldn't-melt mouth and wide innocent blue eyes and perfectly ironed hair (there's another one who's clearly not having to babysit anyone or having to help with washing-up!) is working at *Wicked*. And she's not going to have to fetch coffees – seems I'm so good at that she gets off from having to do anything so menial. Her mum's Alice's best friend, apparently. Well, her home life must be a blast then, with old Alice the boss dropping in for tea after a long day at the office!

But it gets worse – if you can imagine such a thing . . .

Bad news item TWO . . . Rebecca showed me a page of Sean's blog she'd printed off. You'll never guess what? He's only gone and put there in black and white and every other colour of the rainbow what I think of Alice!

HOW COULD HE?

How could he have been so stupid? I mean, he's my friend. Of course I tell him things. But in confidence, right? I don't expect him to go splashing my views on my boss all over the Internet. I mean my dad works for *Wicked* too. We could both get fired. I can describe the woman as having a face like a cat's bum between you and me but you aren't going to tell anyone! But a BLOG????????
That's asking for trouble! Especially when someone like Rebecca turns up with the page printed out to be left whenever she feels like it on Alice's desk.

So that's the last time I tell anybody anything. Privacy. On the surface I shall be bland and non-committal. Inside, I'll keep my seething to myself. I mean, I've been here nearly a month already and this is what I've achieved . . .

Friends? ONE! Jill – the smiley lawyer-to-be with a social conscience – cool, kind, music-minded Jill. Seriously, I bet she ends up a high-court judge one day.

And it'll be, 'All rise for her honour, Judge Jill of Peckham Rye.'

I can't even decide what I want for breakfast, let alone how to make a career out of my pretty random talents with computer design and customizing SMAW's best Issey Miyake! I like the idea of doing an art foundation course in Paris and then getting a job at a French design house. But that's a bit like Devil Child saying he wants to be an astronaut: it's just not going to happen, is it? Besides, if I don't like the people who work in a fashion magazine in London, imagine what the people working in fashion houses in Paris might be like? All that stress over the length of a sleeve.

But back to Sean. He can go JUMP as far as I'm concerned. That's the last time I'm taken in by that Labradorial charm.

14 April

What is it about the adult world? It's not what they say it should be. We young people must be honest and try hard; we must be kind, thoughtful, truthful. Adults can be scheming, manipulative, anything they like to get anything they want.

And my dad can't get anything out of me so he sends me to a counsellor, a total stranger, who I'm supposed to reveal my innermost thoughts to – like if I don't trust my dad I'm going to trust a total stranger!

I mean, he seems nice enough. The counsellor, I mean. But he would, wouldn't he? And it's just like in the films too. I sit on a couch. He has an upright chair. He sits legs crossed, pad at the ready to write down anything he thinks might get me sectioned.

He doesn't say a single word but just waits. I'm supposed to not be able to bear the silence and start blurting out rubbish just to fill the silence.

Well, I didn't. We just stared each other out for an hour, breathing, sighing a bit sometimes, shifting in our seats. He looked much more comfortable than I felt. Me in the middle of a sofa – no, I didn't lie back on it. And him with his back to the light so I couldn't see what his eyes were doing. Trust him?!

At one point the counsellor brought up the subject of drugs. I told him I don't do them. Like it's any of his business – but I don't.

Then he goes, 'What makes you so unhappy when you should be having the time of your life?'

I didn't give him the satisfaction of seeing me cry.

15 April

You know how you think people are, like, seriously sorted, and then they come at you out of the blue and tell you their life stinks almost as much as yours? The problem is, I don't know what to do about it.

Conundrum.

ANOTHER conundrum.

So, I was just, like, hanging out with Sean . . .

YES, I've forgiven him for that stuff he wrote about Alice on his blog. He was so hangdog-puppy-dog about it. And so far Rebecca doesn't seem to have shown Alice anything. Maybe she's just the threatening type? And it's not like I've got so many friends here I can go dumping them at the first opportunity.

Anyway, so I'm just hanging with Sean in the park. He's making me laugh, telling me how he's going to move to LA and be a music producer and make millions and fly me and Jill out there to live in his cool Beverly Hills house with a studio at the bottom of the garden and hot and cold running servants to indulge our slightest whim.

When suddenly, out of nowhere, Jill appears like a storm and drags me away muttering something about girl stuff to Sean and leaving him to daydream about his future successes all by himself.

I won't say I wasn't intrigued by her insistence.

And she didn't make me wait long.

'I need two hundred and fifty quid,' she says, quick as you like. 'Can you get it for me by Thursday?'

What? Like I'm some kind of bank or something?

No! Is the answer to that question. Of course I don't have two hundred and fifty anything and, if I did, would I get it for someone who wouldn't give me a reason, however much they promise to pay it back?!

She said, 'You've gotta trust me, Sofia.'

She said I was the only person she could ask, and that she can't tell her mum or her brother.

And then the penny dropped. I can only think of one thing that she might need that kind of money for. But then why won't she tell me? I could help her. She could see the school counsellor. Jo had a scare last year but in the end that's all it was, a scare. The school were great, though.

What must Jill be going through right now? I mean, when did it happen? Must have been before I turned up on the scene because there's only been a distant fancying of Scratch as far as her love life's concerned while I've been around.

Well, that's all I know so far. She must be going through hell at the moment. I want to help my friend. It's just a question of how.

Isn't that what friendship's about? A true friend would get her the money no questions asked. I mean, I could. I've got it in an account in my name, building up week by week from the work experience so I can pay for the damage at my old school. Is Jill's need not greater than the chemistry lab's? I could get the money for her.

Should I?

16 April

This would be a good time to have the kind of mum you can ring and talk things over with.

But back to the trust question. For lack of anybody else to talk to I MENTIONED IN PASSING to Tom the counsellor that I have this mate Jill, and she's asked me for this money and I think she's pregnant and what should I do? He is quite good at this. He sits there like a kind of receptive brick wall and makes me talk and talk and talk until I reach my own conclusion.

Is that what all counsellors do? Anyway, if that's the case I was really beginning to see the point. I mean, if I'm going to have to see him all the time then I may as well talk to him, right? And if he lets me work things out at my own pace . . . it's like talking to you, only with a bit of encouraging feedback from time to time.

But, hey, guess what? Just as I open up to him and begin to think that counselling might not be a total waste of time, THIS happens: I'm sitting at home playing happy families with Dad, SMAW and Dylan. And Dad and SMAW start harping on about communicating and that if I have problems I should feel free to talk to them. I thought the whole point of seeing a counsellor was that it let them off the hook in that department!

And then it dawned on me. Tom told them. He talked to SMAW and SMAW talked to Dad and now they think it's ME with the problem.

I'm not pregnant!

I thought seeing a counsellor was supposed to be confidential!

I mean, didn't Tom have to swear the Hippocratic oath or something that he wouldn't go round divulging all this clients' business to any dad or SMAW who asked him? TRUST??????????????

It's enough to make me go straight to the drawer where the cash card for the savings account where that money I earn at *Wicked* is kept. Jill can have the money. I trust her. She needs it. She asked for it. She came out clear and honest that she couldn't say why. What would you do?

I stole the bank card. I got Jill the money. I gave it to her.

Dad found out. He's so angry he said he might have to phone my mum.

I couldn't tell him. I promised Jill. I'm not the sort to grass on a friend.

What's Dad going to do? Chuck me out? Send me back to my mum's? She doesn't want me. Maybe I'll have to leave school. Get a flat – how? Persuade *Wicked* to make me a full-time office junior?

I don't love it here but it's all I've got. I've made this room the little ship I sail alone through life in. It's my sanctuary, my safe place – the place where I withdraw to to lick my wounds. I'd love it if I went back to Stockport. Except Trisha would be there. And at home in Stockport my room wasn't as good as this one. This one's all lined in wood, which gives it a cabin feel, and it's high up and looks out over trees. I can't see rooftops unless I climb up and look down and if I'm lying in bed it's like I'm sailing through clouds.

Please don't make me leave.

I feel like I belong in this room – and I sure don't get that belonging feeling anywhere else.

When Dad and Mum line up against me . . . They don't exactly get on so they don't even listen to each other, let alone me . . .

Still, I did the right thing by Jill.

And they can chuck me out if they like and I won't get any A levels and will be an office junior for the rest of my life but, hey, I've soooooooooooooooo got the moral high ground.

18 April

I was desperate. Driven to it. Dad is so mad with me I thought he'd throw me out. And then I went into work and Rebecca and Josh were like all over each other and it just made me feel sick. And there wasn't so much for us work experience girls to do so I spent half the day obsessing about Jill, Dad, Mum, me being chucked out, life on my own . . . Going round and round in circles and getting nowhere.

And, eventually, not long before I actually exploded, I took my life in my hands and I called my mum, hoping against hope that Dad hadn't got to her first.

I was shaking when I dialled the number. I nearly lost my nerve and put the phone down. It was like: she won't speak to me, she doesn't love me, I'm not her daughter any more. But when she finally picked the phone up and I said, 'Mum, it's me . . .' she was so happy I'd called her! I could hear she was almost in tears. She's been waiting for me to phone. She didn't want to get in the way of me settling in. It's not that she doesn't love me, she just didn't want to hold me back. She wanted me to make a success of my new life. She knows how I hate change and she thought it would be good for me to go to my dad's, take me out of myself, widen my horizons.

And then she said, 'It's your birthday soon, love. Why don't you come home to Stockport for a few days and we'll have a party for you?'

She wants me to go back to Stockport for my birthday! I could take Jill and Sean with me. Show them around. They could meet Jo. They know all about each other. It'd be cool, no? My birthday would rock!

In the end, I never told Mum about the Jill conundrum. Dad clearly lost his nerve and didn't call her. She can be quite scary at times; you do have to be desperate to confront her.

I love her.

21 April

Here's something I've learned: secrets always come out in the end.

Jill told me everything.

She wasn't pregnant.

She had this boyfriend called Sy. And she let him take, like, nudie photos of her.

WHAT????????????????

He told her the photos would be like art. Poor girl. She was in love with him. She had a relationship with this guy. She thought she knew him. She trusted him. And NOW look what he's done!

When they split up she ended it and he was really upset. And then he started saying he was going to put those photos on the web unless she paid him. That's what the money she wanted from me was for – hush money!

So much for love and respect, eh?

But even if she had paid him . . . It wouldn't have worked, would it? Might have shut him up for a little bit. But he'd still have the disc or the memory stick or something. He could come after her any time for more.

She must have been so scared and desperate. But in the end she told her brother, Mikey, and he went round to Sy's place and managed to delete the photos from the computer and destroy the memory card and all that. But Jill still doesn't know if Sy made copies. Like in twenty years' time or something, when she's a high-court judge, those pictures might still come back and bite her!

So in the end Dad was cool. I got the money back and gave it to him. And he came up to my room to see if I was all right and I told him everything.

Turns out Tom had told him and SMAW because he really had thought that I was saying that *I* was pregnant. He thought I looked pale and wan and he put two and two together. He thought I was coming out with the old euphemistic 'I've got a friend who's in trouble' line.

OK, that's fair enough then, that he told Dad. I mean, I must have sounded really mad to Tom if that's what he thought. I reckon my dad's just relieved nobody's pregnant. He understood I felt I had to help my friend. He didn't even take the opportunity to give me one of his 'Well, what you can learn from this, Sofia' type lectures. He just gave me a hug.

22 April

That Josh, he so loves himself. He and Rebecca were canooooooooodling in the office today, practically copping off in public (!), while I took a majorly important coffee/cappu/latte/who-gives-a list from Alice. If Alice hadn't been there I'd have told them to go and get a room!

I mean, in the office! EEEUUURRRRGGGGGGHH-HHHH!!!!!!!!! Rebecca was almost drooooooling and Josh loves himself so much he just took it all like it was no more than he deserved.

Still, I nearly laughed out loud when he dropped her like a hot potato when I set off to fulfil this majorly important coffee order. He came along with me, offering to help. Rebecca looked like she'd been slapped in the face. I danced down the stairs to the coffee shop. I mean, I don't fancy the bloke (well, I do but he's such a slime-ball!) but I'd do anything to rain on her parade, the witch.

You know the other day she put on her blog 'Jailbird or jailbait – you decide' next to a picture of Jill. I could have ripped every single perfectly ironed hair out of her over-made-up head!

Anyway, so now it's Josh's turn to be all over me like a rash. He doesn't fool me but it's nice to be paid a little attention for once. He started with, 'You're too clever to be working at *Wicked*.'

And in return for this compliment? He wants me to go into my dad's email account and reply to a mail he (my dad) will get from Alice asking for a recommendation for a shoot this Friday. Josh wants me to pretend to be my dad and say something like, 'Yeah, Josh is cool, I've seen his book. He's just what you're looking for.'

Help him or not help him?

1. I haven't ever had a deck at Josh's precious book. I've got no idea if he's any good as a photographer. But Rebecca's seen it, the witch.

2. Still, he IS seriously cute to look at. If I helped I might get smiled at from time to time, and that really lifts the heart on a day long on coffee orders.

3. And what harm could pretending to be Dad do? I mean, it's true, Josh has been at *Wicked* for, like, MONTHS so he can hardly be a terrible photographer, and he assists all the time on shoots and always takes the in-house shots.

4. And Josh says it's ONLY a press junket. It's not as if Alice needs Nick Knight on this shoot, is it?

5. But then . . . I've only just made peace with my dad. It's, like, hardly brilliant planning to go ahead and abuse his trust AGAIN – even if he is as unlikely to find out about it as Josh thinks.

Dilemmas, dilemmas . . .

6. AND it's not as if my list of friends is getting any longer. In fact it seems to have stagnated at two.

7. But would Josh be more of a fiend than a friend? How great would he be to have around?

8. THIS IS THE BIG ONE! Josh promised to take me to The Script at Koko if I did this for him. I would soooooooooooooo love to see them play.

23 April

Dad's been a photographer all his career. He must be good at it. It's not easy to make a good living freelance, he says. He says you have to keep up your contacts all the time, and constantly get your work looked at by people who might be interested. So sometimes he takes kind of boring shots for jobs I wouldn't necessarily leap at . . . CATALOGUES!!!!!!!!!!!! So my dad's NOT Nick Knight. But, he says, he doesn't have to sit behind a desk all day. His work changes all the time. He travels, meets new people. Works hard but at his own pace. I could think of worse things.

And he takes gorgeous pictures of his friends and family. Like really lovely, classically styled black and white portraits . . . Mum's still got one. It's a shot of me and Mum. I must have been about two years old. We're sitting on a bench on top of a hill looking over a city. She says it's London somewhere. I haven't recognized the place yet. It's all grainy from the slow light and full of wintry atmosphere. She says she kept it because it told a timeless story about people living in the city. Dad's got another one that must have been taken the same day. It's a close-up of a very serious faced little girl with curly hair and a face pinched with cold. I'm looking straight into the camera. It's winter but I still manage to have a few freckles. It's hanging in his office. He's a good photographer.

I hope I inherit both those photos some day. It's good to look at them and remember that once they loved each other enough to have me. Before she moved back to

Stockport so her mum could help look after me when I was little. Before they split up. Before it all went sour.

I asked Dad how he got his breaks. He said, 'Hard graft and sticking at it.'

He said he spent years assisting and learning his craft. He says if you get too high up the greasy pole too quickly you're bound to slip down suddenly when you realize you don't really know what you're doing.

What shall I do about helping Josh? Shall I even mention him to my dad? I mean, he COULD look at Josh's book and IF he likes what he sees THEN he could recommend him. Isn't that what Josh should do? Not try to get in through the back door but call my dad himself and show him his work?

But I would DIE to see The Script . . .

24 April

You know what? I think Josh lives in a dream world where nothing ever goes wrong and he always gets the big break without having to try at all. Those eyelashes of his must have got him through sooooooooooooooo many scrapes.

I nearly did it. I nearly lied for him. I can't believe the eyelashes nearly got *me* too!

There was a fracas to do with SMAW feeling tired and emotional (nothing new there then), Devil Child acting up (ditto) and Dad running around sorting everybody out while he was supposed to be shooting at some house in Bromley with really unusual decor for something stunning like 'Curtains Weekly'.

Anyway, taking advantage of the lull in attention on difficult old me, I slipped into his office and checked his email. Alice *had* emailed him about recommending someone for Friday. But turns out Josh was lying through his over-polished pearlies! It's, like, a MAJOR shoot and not just any old junior underling like Josh Angelo, eyelashes or no eyelashes, could be recommended for it.

I shut the laptop and turned away and I even went so far as to get Devil Child some juice just to remove him from my poor dad's frazzled hair. SMAW all the while lying back on the sofa, of course – back of hand to brow like she's fading away from a nineteenth-century wasting sickness. She's just bored of endless childcare if you ask me – and frankly, I don't blame her!

And as for Josh? He can work his way up like my dad did. If he's any good he'll get somewhere. If all he has are eyelashes to impress with then he'll drop by the wayside as we all dance past waving 'BYEEEEEEEEE-EEEEEEEEEEEE!!!!'

And The Script? You know what they say, 'What goes around comes around.'

Maybe my good behaviour will be rewarded by Script tickets coming to me some other way.

What?

In my life?

You've got to be kidding – right?

25 April

This is how the nasty people keep their egos so bright and shining. They hang out together, tell each other lies about how brilliant they are, believe the rubbish they spout and then take each other to see The Script at Koko. That's Rebecca the Witch and Josh Angelo today. I just hid under my desk and prayed for five o'clock.

I mean, I've got homework! I am doing A levels – or has everybody forgotten that? So's Rebecca but she clearly doesn't care. I shall spend the time THEY waste dancing at Koko getting ahead with my reading, doing some research, being MUCH MORE PREPARED than she'll ever be and get a load of A grades and a place at my first choice of red-brick university, where the music scene is really happening, and where I shall shine, cool AND clever. I will!

Promise.

Well, I might veg on the sofa and watch *Casualty* first . . .

Best-case scenario: Dad and SMAW will take advantage of me being home on a Saturday night, pay me in pizza to babysit . . . and I could ask Jill and Sean over. Maybe Jill won't be able to come? Maybe Sean and I could . . .????

Nah! We're just mates. Aren't we . . .?

Who needs Josh and cool gigs to have a good time?

Sometimes I can make myself sound soooooooooooooooooooo sorted!

Now I don't know what to do. Emergency SMS, Messenger and email to Jo, who, because it's her birthday, is off somewhere out of range of my desperate calls for help.

Sean's asked me out.

Sean's asked me to the cinema.

Free tickets.

Just me, though, not me and Jill.

He called it a mate date.

What on earth is a MATE DATE????????????????????

I've been on dates, and I've got mates. They've never been mixed up together before.

Going to the cinema with a mate involves lots of popcorn, comfortable clothes, a padded coat you can wear IN the cinema because they're always cold inside, and ice cream – shared because there's no fear of bumping tiny little plastic spoons because you don't care. It involves meeting at the cinema, seeing the film, going home.

A DATE?!?!?! Involves uncomfortable new clothes I think make me look beautiful and cool at the same time – a seriously challenging combination whoever you are. A date involves being collected and, maybe, being dropped home. The film is pretty much irrelevant. It's all about touching arms and wondering whether the dateeee has noticed that your arms are touching. Not daring share popcorn or ice cream because of the threat of touching hands too early in the proceedings. A date involves a pattering heart, and a will-he-won't-he refrain circling endlessly around your head until he does or he doesn't, and the whole thing starts again until you next see him.

That's a date.

So what's a mate date?

Jill says I should just chill my boots and go.

Jill *can* say that: she's not been invited on such an ambiguously titled adventure.

Life and loves of Sofia Taylor – well, you've had plenty of life but, now, hold your breath, you might be about to get a bit of the love bit.

Because if it's going to be a DATE . . . then I have to work out what I think about Sean. And the truth is????

He's seriously cute.

If Josh is like a greyhound – you know, sleek, beautiful, fast, something to admire from a distance, then Sean's more the Labrador type. A mess of thick yellow hair to get your hands in, dopey eyes that look at you all soppy. You just want to hug him, let him hug you, get lost in his great big over-enthusiastic keen-as-mustard loving-you embrace. Josh would be all bones to hug. Sean would be lovely.

And he smells nice. Don't ask me what of. But he does. He smells nice.

And he likes me – an aphrodisiac in itself!

And he has no side. He's like soooooooooooo straight. When he wrote that stuff about Alice on his blog it was stupid but it was keen. And he was devastated when I shouted at him for it. He'll never do anything like that again.

But this isn't a date, is it? It's a mate date. So no need to think about all the above, is there? Get out the padded coat and think about shared ice cream. Or popcorn. No, popcorn always gets stuck in your teeth. But ice cream . . . It's a bit like shared bodily fluids . . . no matter how delicately you spoon your chocca mocca or raspberry crush delight.

It's Jo's eighteenth party tonight. She's going out with her new boyfriend and her parents and all our old mates for a slap-up at a place we've been going to since we were little. Pizza and naff happy-birthday singing with tambourines and candles. I wish me and Sean could be there.

29 April

I'll never tell. It's my secret. Well, yours and mine. My MOST embarrassing moment, and, let's face it there've been a few, was when John and I were falling in love. Yeah, it did happen. Whatever occurred later between him and Trisha, and I'll ALWAYS blame Trisha for that, John and I really fell in love. It was like movie-time. Rose-tinted sunsets and romantic music – in Stockport . . .????
It happens!

So, I thought it was going to be his birthday. That's where the problem started. Jo and I had been talking about what I could do to, like, declare how I felt without being too obvious or anything. He'd been throwing me looks by the lockers at school. He said he liked the way I'd stuck a mix of cool shots and stupid headlines from the local paper inside my locker door. It was a running joke, headlines from the local paper . . . You know, stuff like, 'Cat stuck up tree escapes before fire engines get there!'. Basically, NOT news.

So, there was this vinyl shop we used to go to, and I thought if I could accidentally on purpose meet him there I could present him with a present for his birthday. I made Jo do all the talking. She had to strike up a conversation with him – they didn't even know each other – and find out if he knew this store, and if he did when he'd be there and stuff.

Anyway, it worked. He said he sometimes went there after football on Sundays. So then we had to find out where and when he played. Turned out in a league on Sunday mornings finishing at about twelve.

So, of course, we had to be at the vinyl shop from twelve onwards, right?

We took the bus into town. And we waited. And we waited. And we listened to all the tracks that we could find. We trashed the place. There were records and sleeves all over the shop.

And no sign of John.

I'd got myself into a right lather by this time. You know, football's kind of major in Stockport. Never saw the point of it myself but if it keeps a lad fit . . . We didn't have any money either – only enough to buy a record for John's birthday – and we were starving. We'd taken enough for our bus fares and we'd had a coffee when we got there. By now it was, like, four o'clock in the afternoon and the man running the shop wanted to close up.

So I picked up a single by a cool band I like called The Metros. And I bought it. The man gave me a funny look but handed it over wrapped in a little black-and-white-checked paper bag with the name of the store on it – like a present already. Still no sign of John. I was heartbroken. He didn't like me. I was wasting my time. No point in giving him the record or anything. But Jo said, 'It's his birthday! It can't do any harm to give him a present.'

So the next day I did. I slipped the black-and-white-checked bag with the single in it into his locker through the gap between the door and the bottom. I'd written: 'Happy Mondays (it was Monday!) – love from Sofia xxxxxxx'. I'd written seven kisses before I realized I should hold back a bit. We weren't going out or anything at that stage. Just smiling at each other across a crowded corridor.

Anyway, then I had to hang about looking busy by my locker until he came along and found it. Which he did. He didn't look very birthday. No new shirt or crowd of mates saying anything.

He saw the package.

Picked it up.

Opened it.

Frowned. Turned the record over. Looked back at the front . . .

And then I saw!

It wasn't The Metros single at all!

I don't know how it had happened but he was holding a vintage vinyl single of an ancient band called Duran Duran singing the theme tune to some Bond film that Jo and I had thought was really funny and been dancing around to in the shop. They'd got mixed up!

I died.

I died and wished I could just melt into the ground.

But it was break time and the place was heaving. I couldn't get away fast enough. And then he looked up at me and smiled.

'Great joke,' he said. And then he said, 'I love Bond. Got them all on DVD. Fancy coming round to watch one one day?'

And that was it. I stood there, sweat pouring down my back, flushing furiously, and the mistake had bought me my first date.

Of course I said yes! And then I ran off to the loo to air my armpits before I flooded the corridor with shame. It wasn't even his birthday! I found out later he's actually a Scorpio, not a Gemini. But that was cool because by then we were the hot item and I could splash out on some serious tracks for him – he did have kind of nerdy taste in music, though. I think he really liked Duran Duran!!!!!!

Of course there was also the time I wet my pants in assembly when I was seven – that was pretty embarrassing. But I reckon being taken for a Duran Duran fan when The Metros are more my thing has to be the nadir of my life. Still, John and I went out for almost six months after that. Until Trisha . . .

Alice wants me to write a feature for the magazine about most embarrassing moments. I think I'll keep mine to myself. Aren't journalists supposed to keep their own experience out of their reporting?

30 April

You know what? I'd really like things to happen one at a time, know what I mean? Then I'd have time to work out how I feel about them and react accordingly. Instead I'm just bustled along by life and there's no time for anything. I mean, I'm going out with Sean on a MATE date . . . he's taking me to see *Screaming Snakes* 2 or something – I'm just glad it isn't some sloppy chick flick with pauses for copping off every ten minutes or so – and I haven't time to think about what to wear, let alone how I feel about the fact that every time I see him he tells me AGAIN that it's just as mates, we're just mates, a mate date. So why isn't Jill invited?

And THEN he said did I want to go to The Script with him? He should have split the question.

'Do I want to go see The Script?'

Easy answer – YES, I FLAMING DO!

'Do I want to go to a gig with Sean?'

On what terms?

Another mate date?

It's not clear, that's what I'm saying. And instead of having all the time in the world to work out how I feel about it . . .

This is how any NORMAL teenager would react: they'd

retire to their bedrooms, open their books and moon out of the window with their chin in their hands, not studying for a single solitary second but deciding what to do. They'd have time to try on their entire wardrobe and turn their room into something that looks like 'Garage Sale on Mulholland'.

Me? Oh no. I've got work experience, haven't I? And a feature to write. About most embarrassing moments. This is not only boring but time consuming as well.

And you know what I found out? Rebecca, meanwhile, is getting to interview Danny O'Donaghue. You get that? Danny O'Donaghue!!!!!!!!!! Vocals for The Script. I'd DIE for that opportunity. Why does SHE get that when I get 'What Makes You Sweat?'?

AAAAAAAAAAAGGGGGGGGGGHHHHH-HHHH!!!!!!!!

I'm just going to do it. It's a job. Now my CV reads:

Fashion Assistant

AND

Feature Writer.

I'll get to interview someone cool myself one day. Maybe I'll try to set it up. Maybe I should interview Sean and Mikey NOW so that when they're famous I'm already on the case?????????????????

Mate interviewing mate, of course – in high-heeled silver glitter shoes? I think not. And I still don't know what I'm going to wear to the film.

May

1 May

My mum always says you have to grab the opportunities life throws at you with both hands and hold on to them tight. She says things might not always look promising but that if you keep an eye out you might be able to work out a way to improve them.

So, I'm interviewing a load of very dull, very samey teenagers about their most embarrassing moments. We're all practically asleep it's so boring. They can't even raise a laugh themselves when they think of sweat circles under their arms and all kinds of not very imaginative stories like that. When . . .

IN WALKS DANNY O'DONAGHUE!

He's looking for Rebecca who's down to interview him but I'm not going to let him get away that fast. Oh no! Quick as a flash I ask HIM his most embarrassing moment and he tells a great story about trying to escape to see a Stone Roses gig by climbing out of a window and falling and breaking everything and ending up in hospital. I mean a GREAT story! And I asked if I could use it for my article. And Josh took, like, ten really cool shots of him. And all that before Alice and Witch Rebecca realize we've got him in our opportunistic clutches and rush round to tear him away from us.

I bet a million pounds that Rebecca's interview's all smarmy and oily and she gets nothing new out of him that hasn't been said before. MY article, on the other hand, has a story about this GORGEOUS, INTELLIGENT (have you listened to his lyrics?), CHARMING, SMILEY, COOOOOOOOOOOOOOOOOOOOOL singer – a story that he's NEVER TOLD ANYBODY BEFORE!

I tell you what, SOFIA TAYLOR SOOOOOOOOOOO ROCKS!!!!

Well, Sofia Taylor did rock . . .

Until she went to the movies with Sean.

I so totally screwed up.

I don't know what drove me.

Maybe I hadn't had enough time to think about it?

So, the film was terrible – but funny horror terrible, not completely dead, and we had a great time. Chocca mocca ice cream for me (can't get away from coffee, even when I'm not at work) and popcorn for him – he has his half sweet (at the bottom of the bag) and half salt (at the top). He says getting them to make it like that not only gives you a main course and dessert for the price of one bag of popcorn but they have to scoop it out of the freshly popped stuff, which means you can be sure it isn't stale. Nice tip!

So, we had a good time.

And I wore my puffa coat and it WAS cold in the cinema.

And afterwards we were, like, standing on the pavement and it was that shifty, uncertain moment. And he said did I want to go out for a drink?

And I said no.

And he said he'd walk me home then.

And I suddenly realized this wasn't a mate date at all.
Those puppy-dog eyes . . . I could have drowned in them.
He stepped towards me. He reached out . . .

And what did I do? I stepped back, practically into the
road.

And what did I do? I pushed him away.

I said, 'Let's just be friends.'

I said, 'I don't know how long I'm going to be around
for.'

I said, 'I've never had a boy for a best friend before
and I really like it and let's just keep it that way.'

And then I walked off!

I must have been off my head!

Where did all that stuff come from? I hadn't planned
any of it. I'd planned to lose myself in the five-star kiss
I know those lovely big generous lips of his wanted to
plant on me. I meant to cop off with him good and
proper!

And instead I gave him the brush-off.

Sofia Taylor! You soooooooooooooooo do NOT rock!

2 May

And now I'm torn. The worst bit about letting someone
down is the way they look at you all hangdog the next
day. We've ended up avoiding each other. He did it first.
I saw him in the corridor by the lockers and I went to
go and say hi but he saw me and really on purpose turned

his back and high-fived some stranger and went off deep in conversation about a football match. Serious stuff. If he'd been talking about music I might have been able to join in. But he knows I hate football so that was like a double exclusion from his life.

He doesn't want to talk to me.

So, next time I saw him, coming towards me across the grass outside college, I turned aside and pretended to be talking to someone by the bike racks so that he could get past me without having to say anything. This is awful. How long's it going to go on?

And later my mum rang. Of course I picked up! It's not like she and I have such a hot relationship that I dare play hard to get with her. And she still wants me to go home for my birthday. She's going to pay for the ticket and send it to me and everything.

And then I remembered – I said I'd go to The Script with Sean that week. But he won't want to go with me now . . . will he? And I really, really want to see The Script but that's nothing to how much I want to go home.

So then I went and found Sean and Jill in the coffee shop and I sat down and said all cool that my mum wants me to go home for my birthday and I really have to do what she wants because she's going to such an effort and everything. And Sean looks doubly slapped in the face when I thought he'd be glad I can't go to the gig with him. And Jill did her see no evil, hear no evil, speak no

evil expression so there was nothing to be got out of her
– like, HELP ME, FRIEND!

I left them.

I still feel like a new girl in this town.

I'm not going to worry about Sean or Jill. I'm going
to see Mum and Jo . . .

My eighteenth birthday's going to be WICKED!

And it doesn't matter (much) that I seem to be heading
back towards a friend count of ZERO (again!).

5 May

Tom the counsellor wants us to go and see him for a
family session. Like, me, Dad and SMAW on that not-
quite-long-enough-for-three-of-us sofa. Hmmm – Dylan
too? I'm sure he'd have a LOT to contribute.

Tom thinks I'm not committed to my new life.

Too right I'm not.

He says something's got to give or I'm never going to
settle into London. Hey, I'm settled in all right. I just hate
living with Dad, SMAW, Devil Child, and the constant
ambience of Radio 2, that's all.

I like my ROOM. If I could, I'd just have a separate
entrance and a kettle, and we could leave each other
perfectly happy – all alone.

I know that's what SMAW would like. It's hard to be
the blushing bride and yummy mummy with a seventeen-
year-old cuckoo crowding the nest. I feel like I'm the ugly
stepdaughter, and she fancies herself as Cinderella to my
dad's Prince Charming. I feel like I turn the sky in her

permanently pink-sunsetted life a touch too stormy for her liking. And it's not my fault. My existence is the problem, not me.

I mean, it's not like I MEAN to make anybody's life a misery.

Ditto work.

Rebecca keeps accusing me of coming on to Josh.

As if!

We had a good day doing the 'What makes you sweat?' story. I got the great quote from Danny O'Donaghue. She screwed up and was so breathy lovey-dovey to him that she got nothing out of him at all. Hardly my fault. And because Josh and I worked together that day and made not such a terrible team considering we're not exactly bezzy mates, she's jealous.

So, I'm just getting on with work, being a good girl answering phones, taking messages, fetching that all-important tall grande skinny vanilla latte before I'm even asked to, and Rebecca just can't leave the subject of me and Josh alone. I mean I KNOW I don't fancy him. Well, I might FANCY him but I'd never do anything about it because he's too shallow – and I made a pact with myself about shallow men with too many eyelashes for the good of their self-esteem.

6 May

What does she want? That's the big question. I mean, I know she doesn't like me. So what's she after? I'm only enthusiastic about being manipulated if I know what the generosity's buying.

SMAW took me out for a massage and a facial.

And she bought me a gold sequin-covered birthday dress. And gold ballet shoes. It's a kind of Tinker Bell outfit – I LOVE IT!

Whatever it was that was driving her made her love the whole experience too. Chatter chatter chatter like we're the best of friends the WHOLE way through the time we were at the spa.

I've never had a massage before. It was nice . . . Nice? Well, I wasn't THAT comfortable lying on a table being pummelled by a total stranger. My back feels bruised now. But the oil smelt lovely and I nearly fell asleep. After the facial was over the beautician said I might break out in a few days. Thanks a lot! I'm going to Stockport for my birthday covered in acne? Really extra nice.

I don't think that was SMAW's big idea – to ruin my looks for when I go home to Mum. Except, come to think of it, she and Dad don't know I'm going home next week.

She's a bit Jekyll and Hyde with me. I think, when she's got the energy, she has this fantasy that we'll be more like sisters than stepmother and stepdaughter. I mean, she's not THAT much older than I am, I don't think. I know this is hard for her, me living in her house. In fact, she must seriously love my dad to put up with it. Maybe having me live in her house is as hard for her as it is for me.

That doesn't make it any easier to be nice to her. I mean, I'm not a horrible person. I *want* to be nice to her.

It's just, we're so different. She's so . . . GREIGE! We're like chalk and cheese.

So I reckon we're all overdue a break from each other. I reckon Dad and SMAW will be glad to see the back of me for a few days and have the house to themselves.

I'm nervous about going home to Stockport. Whether I like it or not I've got a life here now. Going back to Stockport are they going to think I've changed?

1. Will I look different?
2. Will I sound different?
3. What if I see Jo and we have nothing to say to each other?
4. What if I bump into John?
5. What if he's been going out with Trisha all the time since I've been gone?

There's no way of knowing till I get there. I'm glad I've got my new dress to wear as armour and some new make-up the facial woman gave me. I'll create a mask of powder and eyeliner and smoky shadows: nobody will be able to tell what's going on in my head unless I wish to divulge my secrets.

7 May

I can't wait to get out of here. I got my holiday request form signed by work and Alice made me feel like I was taking serious liberties with my responsibilities. I'm doing work experience not heading up the World Bank!

And then, out of the kindness of my heart, I offered to give SMAW some time off by feeding Devil Child his dinner. Let me just explain about feeding Devil Child. It's an activity that involves so much leaping about entertaining and distracting him that I don't know why SMAW keeps up her gym membership.

So I did the leaping and dancing and the aeroplane business. But no luck. SOMEONE (not me!) had left a bar of chocolate on the table and that's what he wanted. There was no distracting him. No way would he have anything else. So I gave him a piece.

Things I have learned in the past twenty-four hours: DO NOT GIVE BABIES CHOCOLATE WHEN YOU'RE LOOKING AFTER THEM. It makes stepmums go red in the face and start screaming. And that's SO not a good look! All together now: toddlers and tomatoes are OK – no screaming then – but babies and chocolate do not mix. Please learn from my mistakes and you can safely avoid anny-fanatic-lactic shock.

So, you see, however nervous I might be about seeing all my old mates for the first time since forever and a day, NOTHING'S going to stop me getting out of here and on that train for Stockport.

I'm not taking Jill or Sean, though. Well, he's been avoiding me since the disastrous mate date. Jill says he's sold those tickets he had to The Script. Why doesn't he take her to the gig? Or Mikey? Or Scratch even? There are sixty-odd million people in this country: why does he have to be all heartbroken because he's not going out with me? Or, more to the point, why doesn't he try again? I might not run off next time. I might have got used to the idea he fancies me.

Try, Seany! Try!

But until he gets his nerve up it's like there's a great big invisible balloon between us and we can't get past it. If he sees me in a corridor he ducks away like I'm going to shoot him or something. And because he's always rehearsing with Mikey, and Jill's always with Mikey and Sean I'm kind of out of that loop for the moment. I'm glad I'm going home for my birthday.

This whole episode gives me a lot to talk about to Jo too. She's got Karl and Karl is everything to her now. He's fit, he's funny, he likes her . . . Well, Sean's fit as anything and he's really funny, you can't help but laugh at him. And he's got this cool music vibe going, and he cares about things, and when I told him I didn't want to go out with him he was so down about it and now all I want to do is tell him I'm sorry and I made a mistake and can we speed search back to that moment and start over again?

Aim of the day: make up with Sean.

Success so far? ZERO!

8 May

I told Dad and SMAW I'm going to Stockport for my birthday. Expecting them to leap about for the sheer joy of five days off from me, I couldn't believe it when they flipped. Turns out they've been planning all kinds of birthday surprises and now SMAW's all hurt because I won't be there for them.

But what did they expect? Me to, like, not even once think about my EIGHTEENTH BIRTHDAY in advance? It's the most important day of my life so far. I'm hardly going to leave what happens to chance, am I? I mean, even my mum's gone so far as to splash out on a train ticket to get me home – like, NOT cheap!

If I spend my birthday here what's going to happen? Sean will come and lurk in a corner looking all hangdog, and Dad and SMAW will try to tell me what to do, and we'll all have a nice cup of tea and a cake that SHE'S made. And, believe me, she's no queen of the baking machine. She'll make me something she might make Dylan with blue icing and Captain Nemo candles and think it's funny/ironic while I just sit in another corner, far away from Sean, and cry.

It's MY birthday. The ONE day in the year it's supposed to be OK to do what you want, and I have to stay here to make HER feel like she's good at playing happy families?

Well, you know what? I won't.

I even let them come along to one of my PRIVATE counselling sessions with Tom so I could explain in a 'safe environment' – i.e. without them butting in and telling me I'm wrong all the time, and never letting me finish my sentence – why I want to go home to Stockport.

And you know what? *They* need the counselling. *They* interrupted all the time. Me and Tom spent most of the fifty minutes staring out of the window while SMAW and Dad shouted at him about me, shouted over each other, at each other, at me, about how I'm not committing to this new life and how I won't even pretend to play happy families . . . She even brought up the anny-funny-lactic chocolate incident to prove how useless I am with Dylan.

9 May

My dad just made me feel soooooooooooooooooooooooooo bad.

He came up to my room and sat there like HE was the kid about to be excluded and APOLOGIZED! He said he should be angry with my mum for going behind his back and making all these arrangements. He said he really missed me on my birthdays all those years I was in Stockport and had been really looking forward to having me around this time. I guess it would have been a bit of a child's birthday party he and SMAW put on for me – not because that's all she knows how to do (though that's true of course) but because that's what he wants for me. He wants me to be the little girl he missed all those years.

I felt really sorry for him.

But I haven't seen Mum for months.

And if it weren't for the webcam I wouldn't even be able to remember what Jo looks like.

I'm tooooooooooooooooorn!

THEN I went to a party where Mikey and Sean and Scratch – the one I know Jill really has her eye on – were playing. There was a man coming to check them out from Sony BMG and everything. How cool is THAT?

So, Jill and I were there as the groupies. But it turned out we weren't the only ones. Sean has a new hanger-on. A girl called Leah. I reckon she must have been at least twenty or something. I mean, she looked seriously . . . I don't want to say old . . . but . . .

Anyway, Sean didn't introduce her as his girlfriend or anything but he danced with her when he wasn't playing and they left together.

That was a real knife-in-the-heart moment. I haven't felt like that since I found John and Trisha kissing. I must love him. I even like his name. I never used to like the name Sean. I used to think it was a bit naff . . . Now, though . . . it just rolls round my head in a continuous loop . . . Sean . . . Sean . . . Sean . . . Sean . . .

Him going off with Leah . . . it's all my fault!

Why did I give him the brush-off?

I thought he was really hurt. I didn't think he had a line of people he fancied and would just go from me to the next one so fast there'd be no time for me to plan a recapture-the-knight-in-shining-armour campaign.

That's against the rules, isn't it? Shouldn't the rules state that after a brush-off a boy should wait ten days for the girl to change her mind?

Couldn't he tell I was LYING when I said all that stuff about just wanting us to be friends? Couldn't he tell from the way I flush when he flushes and the way I can barely speak to him? Can't he feel the bubble of love growing between us, which will have to be burst by both of us if we're to get together?

Maybe I've read it all wrong.

Maybe if I go to Stockport for a week he'll forget about me.

Or maybe that girl Leah is just a mate . . . She's a bit OLD for him, isn't she? What does she want, a toy boy? Cradle-snatcher. Him and her, it could have been a mate date, couldn't it?

So, question: do I go to Stockport or not?

Reasons to go:

1. See Mum
2. See Jo
3. Reclaim my old life
4. If I don't go, everyone in Stockport will think I don't care about them any more.
5. TO BELONG!!!!!!!!!!

Reasons to stay here for my birthday?

1. Make Dad happy
2. Make SMAW feel like she's not such a wicked step-mother
3. Sean could come to my party and we could kiss and make up????!!!!!

Whatever happens, the new gold-spangled dress will feature as THE outfit.

12 May

I didn't go.

I didn't go home to Stockport.

I'm still here.

I think I'm doing the right thing.

But it's not making me happy. And it's really hard to be gracious about it.

I mean, Alice was so pleased to see me in work when I should have been away she just threw about three hundred lip glosses at me and wants me to choose the best three and write a blurb on them and never mind a half day off for my birthday.

SMAW and Devil Child are downstairs doing whatever you do to make birthday cakes from scratch. I know I should be pleased they're going to so much effort. But now I've gone through the emotional trauma of not going home to see Mum and Jo I feel, like, completely deflated. I don't even care about Sean any more.

I feel like acting all spoilt, stamping my feet and shouting, 'Go on then, prove it was worth my staying here for my birthday in this miserable house with you.'

I feel like crying my eyes out.

The truth is, I always hate my birthday. I hate the pressure to like all the presents and publicly have a good time no matter what. All that expectation just makes me want to scream!

13 May

I got the most amaaaaaaaaaaaaazing present. Josh gave
me a Contax camera. Can you believe that? Maybe I've
TOTALLY misjudged him. I mean, he must REALLY,
REALLY like me to do something like that.

I turned up at work this morning and it was already
on my desk. With a note. It read: 'This was my first
camera. I took my most important photos with it. Hope
you become an addict . . . like me! Love . . .'

And he didn't sign it or anything but who else could
it be? LOVE????!!!!

Really?

I didn't think he had eyes for me. I thought those lashes
were all for himself. It's so generous! Maybe it was a
freebie and he didn't want it . . . no, you'd keep a Contax.

I don't know. This turns everything on its head. I mean,
I HAVE to reassess Josh now, don't I? I can hardly accept
this present and not take a fresh look at him, can I?

1. He's gorgeous – undeniable.
2. He's seriously generous – unexpected.
3. Is he still as shallow as a puddle on a miserable
   January morning? Perhaps I ought to try to find out.

14 May

It wasn't Josh who gave me the camera.

I feel so awful I just want to curl up in my floating-
away bedroom and die!

They tried. Dad and SMAW made such an effort to

give me a birthday to remember. I could see how proud my dad was that I was his little girl. I could see all the effort SMAW had gone to making that enormous cake and everything. And there were candles and people were snapping away – I was snapping away . . . But when they sang 'Happy Birthday' – Sean, Jill, Josh, everybody, even Dylan joined in a bit – clapping and dancing, suddenly I couldn't bear it. I couldn't bear that I wasn't at home with my mum and Jo and my old mates. And I ran off up here to my room so they wouldn't see me cry. After all, I'm eighteen now. I shouldn't just break down in tears because I can't cope with emotional pressure. I'm not a child. I'm not my dad's little girl. I never was . . .

I should have gone home to my mum.

And it turned out it was my dad who gave me the camera, not Josh. It's my dad who hopes I take after him and have an eye for a good shot. How could I have got THAT so wrong? He must have left it in the office and asked Alice to put it on my desk that morning. What a lovely present. I'm soooooooooooooo touched by it. And much better that my dad gave it to me instead of Josh. Josh being so generous was confusing to say the least!

And Dad and SMAW *did* make an effort. The party was perfect – for somebody else. It wasn't their fault I got so upset. I was in the wrong place. I made the wrong choice. What was wrong was that I wasn't home with my mum. They couldn't have magicked her out of the sky, could they? Maybe we could all have gone to Stockport and all have been together for my birthday? No, that was never going to happen.

I don't know WHERE I belong.

15 May

Pragmatism. Now there's a word. It's something I must learn, I think, if I'm to survive anywhere. It's something people who join the Foreign Office and go off to run embassies in Turkmenistan have to practise. It's something the good ones – the good ambassadors, I mean – got to practise a lot during that ancient conflict, the cold war.

A levels . . . They're really all about learning to deal with your family.

At the moment I am enemy and spy at the same time.

Enemy of? SMAW. Battleground? Dad.

And are we having a good, honest-to-goodness all-out war with nuclear warheads exploding in the kitchen? Of course not. It's all backbiting, behind-the-scenes stuff, needling negotiation for quality time – she with him, me OUT OF HERE! – with bribery and corruption rife.

Given that I HAVE to live somewhere . . . and, having thought hard about it, given that I LIKE studying more than I like the idea of getting a full-time job and trying to find a studio or a flat share or something, then I'm going to have to make myself agreeable.

You hear a lot when your room's at the top of the stairs, above the landing, right at the top of the house. I reckon sound rises as well as heat. She's really had it with me. And I'm going to have to do something to negotiate a peaceful treaty or this house will explode.

It's all about working out your priorities in the end, I've decided. Do I really want to go home to Stockport? Well, if Trisha weren't there I would. But, for the moment, home in Stockport means sharing a house with Trisha. And, on balance, I think I'd rather share a house with SMAW.

Dad's given me tickets to The Script for my birthday. He says they're from SMAW too. A pragmatist would read the cue he's giving me there and accept them with a real-life smiley face and thank HER.

16 May

I may be right about everything but that doesn't mean I have to rub how wrong she is in her face all day long, does it? The moral high ground can be a lonely place sometimes.

OK, so I'm in a seriously good mood.

I did the daring.

No! Not apologize to SMAW – though I did that too – just cos my heart was bright and glittering with hope.

So, Jill and I were hanging out over coffee. I asked her to go with me to The Script. She can't. Her mum and her nan are doing some great annual cook-off in memory of her dad. Fair enough.

But who am I going to see The Script with then? I can hardly take my dad, can I? And Josh is just a slimeball. Of course, we all know who I REALLY want to invite to go with me. But do I have the nerve to ask him? I mean, he was OK at my birthday but I wasn't. I, like, totally lost it and he probably thinks I'm a complete weirdo because of that! And I couldn't ask him out, could I? I don't think I could keep a straight face if I said 'mate date'. Besides, I don't want to go on a mate date with him. I want this to be a proper date. I mean, of course I want to see The Script too . . . but if I could go with Sean . . . It would be soooooooooooooooooo cooooooooooooooool!

Well, let me tell you how much I LOVE Jill. She just did all my dirty work for me. Just like Jo would have done in Stockport. That girl's a proper mate – a reliable, helpful, initiative-using mate.

So, back to the beginning:

Jill and I are just hanging out over coffee, and guess who walks in?

Sean!

And I'm just tongue-tied. And he keeps hitting me – you know, in a punch-on-the-shoulder-for-no-good-reason sort of way – surely a sign he still fancies me . . .??? I mean, there's been no sign of that girl Leah since the gig the other night.

So, does he? Fancy me, I mean! Do you think when a boy punches you on the shoulder all the time it's because he likes you?

Anyway, so I'm all tongue tied and blushing until trusty old Jill just steps in and translates for me.

She asks him if he wants to go to The Script with me.

And he says . . .

YES!!!!!!!!!!!!!!!!!!!!!

LALALALALALALALALALALALALA!!!!!!!!!!!!!!!!!!!!!!!!!

I'm so HAPPEEEEEEEEEEEEEEEEEEEEEEEEEE I could FLYYYYYYYY out of my lovely bedroom window and scoot around the whole neighbourhood dropping swirls of glitter all over everyone to cheer them up.

So, when I got home from that fantastic experience, warm with the hope of a trip to The Script with old Seanybabes, of course I was nice to SMAW. It cost me nothing to apologize. It's easy to be pragmatic when you're happy. Poor woman, she has to live with me, my dad and Devil Child and, as far as I know, has nothing to look forward to herself.

I, on the other hand, am going to see The Script with the hottest boy I know.

There wasn't even talk about whether it was a date, or a mate date, or anything. He just looked at me and said, 'We're cool.'

And I know that means he understands what's been going round and round my head, and I think something similar's been going round and round his too.

EEEEEEEEEEEEEE!!!!!!!!!!!!!!!!!!!!!!!!!!!!!!!!!!!!!!

19 May

Seems like I've been making resolutions on my birthday forever! And they last no longer than the ones I make at new year.

This year my birthday list went like this:

1. Stop wasting time.

But then I thought about it: I'm so busy with school and study and work and babysitting and helping with Dylan and the laundry and the house and everything – if I get five minutes to slob out in front of the TV then I reckon I've earned it! Tom says 'me' time's always valuable. You have to recharge your batteries some way or other. So that's THAT resolution out the window.

2. Chuck the peanut butter and cheese.

It's an odd combination, I know. Better than my grandpa, my mum's dad, who was evacuated to America during the Second World War (NOW we're talking HISTORY!). He used to eat peanut-butter-and-jam sandwiches. Eeeeuuuurrrggghhh! And I'm a growing girl who needs calcium for her bones and peanut butter to stop her nails splitting. Seriously!

3. Say what I mean.

To Alice? I wouldn't have a job! And now I'm practising pragmatism, I can't say what I think to SMAW or Dad most of the time either. If I said what I thought to Sean I'd be putting my heart on the line and my poor battered little heart's too precious for that. So, for the moment,

I'll say what I mean in my academic homework and everything else can remain private. Except between you and me. I'm never anything but straight with you!!!

4. Give London a chance.

Do I have to???? It's so crowded, that's the thing I really hate. And nobody EVER says anything to you unless they have to.

Back to the resolutions:

5. Get to know Dad.

Now THAT one's going to take more than tickets to The Script. It's not that I want him to buy my friendship. It's just that it really is as if I've come to live with a stranger. He and my mum get on, like, really, really badly. They have as little to do with each other as possible. Which means historically, like, during my entire life, I'VE had as little to do with him as possible. Now I can blame him for letting my mum push him away, or I can blame my mum. Either way, he's still a stranger.

We don't even look alike. He's got this new life, this new family. I'm like a lodger here or something, only unlike a straight commercial agreement, I pay my rent in emotional pounds of flesh. It's exhausting. And it's really difficult to think any other way than that he's going to have to earn my trust just as much as he harps on about me earning his.

I did make up with SMAW, though, which wasn't on my list but which I reckon is a big enough deal to cancel out all the dodgy failings with the above.

OK, so she's not THAT awful. Yes, she wears greige all the time. Yes, she's decorated her house entirely greigely. And yes, I WILL help her find some colour in her life.

You know that night she took me for the massage and the shopping, she really tried. And she might be the worst cake maker in the world but she really tried with my birthday too. Some people might have just thrown money at the situation. But she went for it with the time thing too: and she doesn't have much time, especially when I'm her date and so not there to Dylan-sit for her.

I've realized that with her it's not about endless successes, it's about the fact she never stops trying. I mean, she's NOT the brightest spark in the box. She's really never going to be Kate Moss. And yet she struggles along, trying to be all things to all people. It's not make-up, those black rings under her eyes. It's exhausting trying as hard as she does all the time to get everything right.

Maybe I should make a new resolution: don't be so judgemental of SMAW for not succeeding. Appreciate the fact that at least she makes an effort . . .

Maybe . . .

Saw Sean playing football this afternoon. He's good at it. Football, I mean. Better than John was, I reckon. Though I try to keep out of football on principle. That's another thing I've got handy for psychology: how football has replaced the urge to go to war in the still essentially animal male of the species. Maybe I WILL do psychology at university?

Anyway, I saw Sean. And it was cool between us. I mean, he came to my birthday party and didn't sulk about the place like a black cloud.

I like it that we're past the bubble of whatever it was between us. I like it that we're at the uncertain place again. I don't want to get any further. I like not knowing. This way I can imagine any outcome I like. Once we've kissed . . . if we kiss . . .

20 May

I'm obsessing about him. It's not healthy.

It's even got to the stage where Witch Rebecca was ordering me about at work, like I'M her slavegirl or something, and the fantasies about pouring hundreds of cups of sugar-free vanilla lattes all over her perfectly ironed hair were cut short because I had to check my phone to see if I'd missed a text from Sean – unlikely, he NEVER texts me. It's Jill who makes all the social arrangements between us. He just tags along with whatever she wants to do.

And she does what Mikey wants. She's seriously in thrall to her brother, that girl.

Now there's a family. If I were an anthropologist I'd do a study on Jill and all her relations cos it's so alien to anything I've ever known. You know, a close-knit family all living up and down the road from each other, in and out of each other's houses, eating dinner together all the time. Dad, SMAW and I are like ships in the night. Maybe one night a week we manage to eat together. And we're anything but close.

Still, right now I don't care about work. I don't care about Rebecca or Alice. I don't even care about my averagely awful dysfunctional family. I don't care about anyone or anything so long as I'm going to The Script with Sean, the fit, footballing, keyboard-playing boy!!!!!!!!!!!!!!!!!!!!!!!!

21 May

I kissed him. I kissed him. I KISSED HIM!

Last night was, like, the most amazing night of my whooooooole life. Last night should have been my eighteenth. In fact, I bet, when I'm an ooooooold woman and look back on my youth I'll remember last night as being my eighteenth. I'm going to blank what happened last week. Those tickets were a GREAT present, Dad! And Jill, THANK YOU for asking Sean to go with me. And Sean . . . Thanks for just being the most adorable you!

YOU'RE SOOOOOOOOOOOOO GREAT!!!!!!!!!!!!!!

Maybe it was the high-heeled glittery silver shoes that did it? I'll never know. But something gave me courage and I MADE THE FIRST MOVE! We were on the balcony, looking down at the band and the crowd was going wild and the sound was amaaaaaaaaaaaaaaaazing! And we danced and we laughed and we couldn't hear a word the other said, so in the end, instead of trying to tell him how cool I think he is I just grabbed his face and kissed him! Eeeeeeeeeeeeeeeeeeeeeeeee!!!!!!!!!!!!

Whatever came over me? I don't know where the bravery came from but I just couldn't wait any longer. I HAD to know what it would be like. I HAD to know if he'd reject me. But no rejection, he just kissed me right back.

For a while.

I can't believe I have to concentrate at work tomorrow. I can't believe I have to think about ANYTHING else. Because here's the conundrum: at the end of the kiss, which did, like, seriously, go on for about an hour and a half, he said, 'We'd better not, Sofs.' He has this really cute, goofy way of calling me Sofs.

So, 'We'd better not, Sofs'. What's THAT supposed to mean?

I can't sleep for going over and over it in my mind. I've got a kind of constant replay of scenes since we met going through my head on a loop. When he gave me my phone back in the school corridor . . . When I went to that first party and he danced with me . . . When he took me to the cinema and I gave him the brush-off . . . Is THAT what this is about? Is it because I said no last time? I mean, I didn't MEAN it! Surely THAT'S clear enough now. And it took us soooooooooooooooooooooo long to get over that – like, WEEKS. And now . . . I kissed him and he kissed me back and then he said, 'We'd better not.'

I can't wait to find out what Jill thinks. I mean, Jill's known him for, like, years and years. They were even at primary school together. He's Mikey's best friend. He's Jill's best friend. She'll explain. Well, I can hardly ask HIM to explain himself, can I?

I can't believe I've got to work tomorrow. And I've got to DO stuff for Rebecca, like she's my boss or something! Well, I FORGOT to do it today. She should learn how to send stuff over to the printers herself. I'm not her secretary. I might well find I'm too busy to help her out tomorrow at all!

22 May

Well, Jill was no help. She told me to ASK Sean what he meant by 'We'd better not'.

I can't do that! I can't ask him straight out why he pulled away from our kiss. He mustn't know how much I mind. He mustn't think I'm desperate. He's got to seek ME out and explain. If I see him around I've got to run away in the opposite direction – looking cool and like I couldn't care less, of course.

Oh, it's so complicated!

Maybe there should be an A level in this. You know, a set of rules you learn and then people stick to. Then I'd be able to read the signs. Did he mean, Sofs, we'd better not . . . Like, Sofs, I'm not into you and thanks for The Script ticket, it was great but you're not that great.

Or did he mean, Sofs, we'd better not . . . Like he

doesn't want to get hurt, doesn't want to take things too fast, like he wants to make all the running?

How can I find out if all Jill's got to say is, 'Ask him!'

Oh my God! Rebecca's mum's even more po-faced than Alice!

This afternoon I was minding my own business and quietly forgetting to email Rebecca's copy to the printers when this broomstick of a woman stalked into the office, peering down her long aquiline nose as if there were a nasty smell under it. I thought it was the Angel of Fashion Death come to seek me out for wearing last season's trainers.

Anyway, so there's this piece-of-string woman picking her way down the office in spiked heels and it turns out to be Rebecca's mum! I mean, poor girl. Her mum's a total nightmare woman. She was air-kissing Alice and snarling at Rebecca, who just turned into a gibbering wreck while her mum was standing there.

'Doing fine is not enough!' she squawked. 'You have to do brilliantly.' Rebecca quailed.

Hey, don't get me wrong. I haven't changed my spots and started liking the girl all of a sudden. I'm just saying, in a kind of pop-psychology way, I now understand what's driving Witch Rebecca. She's a witch because her mother's a witch to her. She's learned her skills at the cauldron of an expert.

A weaker girl than I would have felt sorry for Rebecca and sent the right file to the printers. A weaker girl would have indulged in a little short-term friendliness with Rebecca and maybe even offered to get her a coffee. But she looked so shaken by her mother's dropping by that I reckoned the last thing she needed was caffeine. And it's really important that she learns that having a horrible mother doesn't buy her gentleness from nice people like me.

She wanted me to send the copy over to the printers because she was too grand to learn how to do it herself. Well, I think she needs to learn not to get so above herself.

I looked at the memory stick with her copy on it. What did she say the file was called? 'Rebecca A'? Or 'Rebecca B'?

Listen, I'm NOT a witch, all right, like she is. But she's gotta learn not to trust people she's been consistently horrible to every day since she met them, i.e. ME – to fulfil her wishes to the letter as if I were some kind of slave. I emailed the printers all right. Because I can. Because I know how. Because I've bothered to learn how to shrink files and get them over there by the deadline. Because she's too grand to do her own editorial house-work.

I'm not sure WHICH file I sent, though. Kind of vague labelling, don't you think? A or B? Surely it would have been cleverer to title her piece 'Rebecca's file' and delete anything that a mistake could have been made with? Don't you think there are about five lessons to be learned here, Rebecca the Witch?

23 May

How can Witch Rebecca expect me to be able to concentrate on HER work (like THAT'S my job anyway!?!) when I've got corridor sightings and strange avoidances and all the uncertainties of a will-he-won't-he love affair to worry about?

Alice had a FIT when the wrong article was printed in *Wicked* and blew Rebecca up sky high. Great. That'll be the last time I get treated like a secretary by somebody who started work experience after I did.

Leaving me to worry about encountering Sean.

I bumped into him in the corridor.

Well, I didn't.

I saw him putting stuff in his locker so I went to turn away but I know he saw me so now he knows I'm avoiding him. So I know he knows I don't know what to do about him. And he knows I know he knows he brings me out in a sweat because he saw me escape to the toilets to splash my face with water and get a hold of myself.

The stress!!!!!!!!!!

He did kiss me back. That I know. Maybe he's really old fashioned and likes to make all the moves. Maybe I should have played harder to get. But last time I played hard to get with him (unintentionally) he went off with Old Woman Leah and we didn't see anything of him for weeks.

I don't know.

26 May

Screwed up again!

I bumped into Sean in a vinyl store I sometimes see him at. I was listening. He was listening. And I didn't notice him. Well, I did but I didn't know whether he'd noticed me. Or whether he was pretending not to notice me and just wanted to listen. And so he turned up whatever he was listening to REALLY, REALLY LOUD and starting singing along REALLY, REALLY BADLY! All goofy, and it was soooooooooooo funny . . . well, maybe you had to be there.

But this is how I screwed it up. He started to try to explain himself.

And I didn't let him!

I mean, how STUPID is that?

Basic psychology. Don't put your hand over a boy's mouth when he's trying to say something and tell him, 'We're cool.'

He took my hand and everything. He looked deep into my eyes.

And I lost my nerve and wouldn't let him speak. I spoke over him!!!

Chatter, chatter, chatter . . . a load of nervous rubbish just to stop him saying whatever it was he wasn't going to say because I had my hand over his mouth. I sounded like SMAW at the spa. Don't tell me SHE was nervous being out with me????

Anyway, back to Sean. I mean, even if that's what I wanted . . . I do want it to be cool between us. I want it to be like it used to be. You know, best friends in the playground stuff. But I want the . . . I want more too. I'm eighteen now. We're not just running around playing tag, measuring friendship in shared Snickers and Haribo Coke bottles. Are we? We're older than that. We need to COMMUUUNICATE as Tom the counsellor would say.

And I've been practising. I can commuuuuuuuuuuuuu-nicate really nicely with SMAW these days. If you didn't know the full story you might think SMAW and I got on with each other, like, normally well. Ditto Dad. But that's easy. That's just pretending in order to keep the peace.

Sean?

It MATTERS that we keep the peace. But it matters too that we say what we mean to each other. And today I stopped that. And that's why I'm really, really dumb.

And he picked up the relaxed vibe and went straight for it. He and Mikey have finished their demo. It's wicked. But I want to know what he wanted to say to me BEFORE that!

And the bad news? (Yes – there IS more, WORSE!!!!, to come.)

SMAW's thinking of going back to work. Catalogue modelling. Paid to sit about looking pretty as a picture all day long. Niiiiiiiiice. And I can TELL who's going to be roped in to help with the childcare.

27 May

Jo reckons Sean's using me.

I don't believe it. Is Jo just jealous? How do *you* read this scenario . . .? I was revising with Jill this afternoon and Sean came and found us. So far so ordinary. Then he's there and he practically high-fives me like we're about to go and play some American football or something.

'We're cool,' he says.

'We're cool?' I reply, and he doesn't realize it's a question – not surprising since I didn't make it sound like one, but anyway . . .

And suddenly – Jo reckons Sean and Jill even rehearsed this . . . I don't believe it.

It went like this: Sean starts. He's like, 'Hey, you could give a copy of our demo to the A & R guy who comes in to *Wicked.*'

'Yeah, that would be soooooooooooooo coool,' says Jill and suddenly she and Sean are dancing all over the place singing stuff like 'Hey Sofia's co-ol. Mikey and Sean are going to be famous. La la di la la.'

And I'm like: 'Who am I to go round giving stuff to A & R guys? I'm, like, lowlier than the photocopying machine at *Wicked.* Why would any A & R guy take a blind bit of notice of me?'

'Because you can pretend to be someone important,' says Jill.

'The A & R guy doesn't have a list of who's who at *Wicked,*' says Sean.

'You could pretend to be the sounds editor,' says Jill.

You can see what Jo means with the maybe-they-rehearsed-all-this vibe.

Me? Pretend to be the sounds editor?!!!!!!!!!!!!!!!!!!!

Won't the A & R guy notice I'm sitting at a trestle table next to the photocopier and the water cooler with an especially large phone so I can answer calls for the whole office and put things through? Won't he notice the piles of rubbish people like to dump on that very desk at any time of the day or night with Post-its stuck to the piles saying things like:

1. File this.
2. Bin this.
3. Get this list of coffees.
4. Crawl, worm!

An editor has, like, their own space and a desk clear other than the tools of their trade that they choose to have around – things I'd love to have at work, like an iPod, and a coffee somebody else brought them.

So, once again . . . dilemma, dilemma . . .

Do I help Sean out?

What does he want?

I don't KNOW!

Jo says be careful.

But she doesn't knooooooooooooooooow him!

Tom the counsellor reckons I've got the post-birthday blues. I haven't got the post-birthday blues! I've got the full-on, full-time, all-year-round miserables.

28 May

I never thought I'd see the day when I said I felt sorry for SMAW.

There seems to be this whole thing that goes on between women with men and women without men. They're so competitive. OK, so here's the scenario: SMAW's friend Alana was coming round for coffee. SMAW totally cleaned up the whole house and had the place looking like something out of a *You* magazine spread. There was the smell of percolating coffee and freshly baked cake and SMAW was in one of her you'll-never-believe-how-much-this-cost-style greige tops and matching jeans and even a pair of boots with heels, which I know she has to squeeze her feet into because I've seen her struggle to do the zip. And during all that preparation time Devil Child played nicely with his trains and a bear and even sat and looked at a book.

But then Alana rang the doorbell and, as if on cue, Devil Child went completely manic. He kept pulling his trousers off and leaving a trail of baby wipes all over the place and generally causing total carnage and all SMAW wanted was five minutes with her old mate, right?

SMAW had baked another of her terrible cakes (competitive showing off, see?) but the other woman, refusing to play, suddenly announced she was vegan, which means no milk in her coffee, no cake because of the eggs (so stalling the showing off) AND she has to watch her figure because, she says, SMAW's in a place where she can afford to let herself go and look old and frazzled. Horrible! This woman was supposed to be SMAW's friend!

But there's the rub. Being friends with people IS about having things in common. If some other woman had come round with a child Dylan's age then they'd have all stuffed the cake perfectly happily, both children would have trashed the place and SMAW would have had a lovely time.

Instead, this Alana woman, who's supposed to be SMAW's great old mate, leaves SMAW in tears because she makes SMAW feel her life's fallen apart and she's become a family woman rather than an independent working woman. And the reason Alana was horrible to SMAW was only because she's jealous of the man and the baby and the house. Alana's on her own.

So I made another pot of coffee and we drank it, and stuffed the cake together and she completely chilled those zipped tight boots and even let Devil Child have some cake, even though it was chocolate!

Ladies who lunch, my pretty backside! Ladies who emotionally punch more like.

I'm gonna see if I can give Sean and Mikey's demo to the A & R guy at work. I'm not promising anything: got my friendships burnt before when I did that. But I'll try.

Why'm I gonna do this?

1. Because I know them.
2. They work really hard.

3. This means a lot to them, and, if I can, I'll help.
4. It's not about me and Sean falling in love. It's about giving the guys a leg up.
5. Jo doesn't know them. She's right not to trust them. She's right to watch my back. But I'm gonna go with what they want. This might be their big break and it would be sooooo great if they made it!
6. My mum always says what goes around comes around, one good turn deserves another and all that. Well, I'm not holding out for any rewards but it's going to cost me nothing much to try. And it might get them everything.
7. And this thing about being friends and choosing alliances. I've chosen these guys to be my mates. I really rate them. It's not all about what you get back from something. Sometimes you've got to help a guy out just because you can.

29 May

I did it. I did it! I'm still shaking.

OK, the guy from Sony BMG was coming in for a meeting with Alice at three. So I hid all the rubbish that litters my desk normally and I wore my customized jacket and lipstick and Pearl Drops and I flashed the A & R man a smile so wide he was blinded by it as he came out of the lift. No bad thing he was blinded – wouldn't have helped if he'd seen WHERE my desk was: right next to the photocopier, the water dispenser and the toilets! Anyway, I shook his hand and looked him straight in the eye and introduced myself as Deputy Music Editor (put THAT on the CV with the fashion editor and the features writer lines!).

And he looked at me straight back and there was no way he didn't believe me. And I gave him Sean and Mikey's demo and he took it and put it in his case and I'll never know if he listens to it – unless he, like, calls them up tomorrow and asks them in for a go-see!

Afterwards, Alice took me aside and gave me such a rollocking! Well, worse actually, she warned me she would give me a rollocking and I've still not heard a word from her so no doubt she's sitting in her den, looking into her cauldron, stewing over my punishment with enormous gleeeeeeeeeeeeeeeeeeeee.

Worse still, Jill had told Sean I was definitely gonna give this guy their demo, which was not what I'd said at all – and Sean turned up at the office at the very moment the Sony guy was leaving!

I mean, SEAN!!!! Leave me alone to do my magic – don't come and screw it up by loafing about in the office like this is something out of *High School Musical* or something.

I mean, this isn't a joke. Sean and Mikey could at least get a talk with the Sony guy out of this. I need to be left alone to do my work without Mr Puppy Dog Eyes bouncing all over the office like an overexcited Labrador.

Still . . . all is not lost. The overexcited Labrador made me a CD of all these tunes he really likes. I like them too. I like him. I still like him even though he's using me to climb the greasy pole to music stardom and he'll leave the likes of work-experience Sofia sooooooooooooo-oooooo far behind he won't remember me in a week or two.

But today . . . Tom says I have to learn to live in the moment and stop worrying about the past and the future so much . . . so, today I have a great CD and Sean wrote on it, 'Thanks, Sofia. Love from your biggest fan.'

Corny. Nice corny? Perfect.

30 May

Jo was right.

Sean's using me.

I'm nothing to him but a step up the ladder to stardom. Seriously.

And I was just allowing myself a tiny little glimmer of hope that helping your friends out was worthwhile!

So, for fun and a change, I was at work – AGAIN! And for fun, and because there was nothing better to do, I took an order for, like, fifteen coffees. And being my usual efficient, effective self I listed them, bought them, paid for them and balanced them precariously on only two trays so that I could get them all back upstairs in one go while they were still hot enough to drink. So I had to turn round and push the door of the coffee shop open with my back because I had no free hands, and what did I see?

Sean having coffee with that Leah girl, that's what I saw!

How could he?

I mean, I thought we were cool. He gave me a CD!!!!!! With 'Love' written on it.

Worst of all, I got such a shock seeing him there I spilt half the coffees all over the steps, ruined my new orange Bensimon plimsolls (not expensive but, like, seriously difficult to source!), made myself look a total fool in front of him AND the hateful Leah, and ran back up to the office fighting tears I didn't want anyone to see. I had to hide in the toilets until I'd calmed myself down because Josh is taking pictures of all the staff at *Wicked* for some naff board idea Alice's got going, just to fill his time, I reckon, and I seriously didn't need photographing with mascara running down my face.

But when I came out of the toilets he still took my picture looking ravaged and hurt and sooooooooooooooooo pissed off I could have snatched the camera and thrown it out of the nearest window if I wasn't being shouted at by Alice because HER coffee was one of the ones that went all over the shop steps and, naturally, it's the end of the world when SHE doesn't get her hourly caffeine fix. I think she should see an addiction counsellor, I really do.

So, bottom line: Sean's seeing Leah. And he's not interested in me.

I have to get over him.

I have to get over this . . . this falling-in-love business.

I have to harden myself up and not be such a softie.

He's not the only guy in the world. It's a big world

and I know practically nothing of it. So, Seanybabes, you might be going to be a megastar of the music firmament but, you know what, what really rocks my boat is the idea of being one of the ones who decides who gets to be a star. That's what I want to do. I want to be the A & R guy. Once I get out of *Wicked*'s not so wicked clutches I NEVER want to be told to get a coffee ever again. I never want to be used for my connections. I want to BE the connection.

June

2 June

This is NOT hot news. SMAW's going back to work. Sitting pretty in lilac cardigans and pressed beige slacks while smarmers like Josh take endless shots of her for catalogues selling clothes to yummy mummies who want to look like her. Sometimes they have little captions telling you a bit about the girl in the photo, something like: Jane likes Chardonnay, champagne and crisps.

Where SMAW's concerned they should put: Emma likes nothing more than playing with her lovely little boy, Dylan.

She, Dylan and her husband Simon are always dressed in GREIGE to match their GREIGE house and their GREIGE lives. The only colour comes from her wayward stepdaughter, Sofia, who's more of a pink and orange kind of girl but who WON'T EVER let herself be made an object in front of a camera.

I wish!

So, SMAW's going back to work and yours truly's going to have to do loads and loads more childcare. Funny how she got over my fear of feeding Devil Child chocolate soon as she got the chance to go and hang about having her hair straightened and her eyebrows plucked in the name of a career. Perhaps I'll do just that. Perhaps I'll feed him chocolate and crisps and E-numbers and Coke until he's so hyper they won't know what to do with him. Perhaps . . .

I know! He's my brother.

Still, at least claiming a need to babysit will give me a reason to avoid Sean. If I could only find out what the REAL story behind Sean and Leah is . . . I don't want to hate him. I don't want to harden my heart against his. I want to be able to fall head over heels in love with the guy, and for him to do the same with me, and for us to swan off into the sunset after our exams – the world our oyster, travelling, making music, choosing what kind of people we're going to be.

3 June

OK, so now I know all about her. She's called Leah Norris. She's a promoter.

I googled her. She's definitely too old for Sean. And their relationship could be professional – though it doesn't look like it the way she looks at him. She's TWO years older than him! I mean, I can see HIS motivation. It's always cool to go out with an older woman, right? If you're shallow enough to be interested in that kind of thing.

It's good. I'm glad me and Sean aren't an item. I'm finding out A LOT more about him. If ever (secret sigh) we were maybe on, into each other again, you know . . . then I'd be going into the whole situation with my eyes much wider open.

There's a party to celebrate Sean and Mikey getting money from Sony to record a demo.

1. Will I be able to get time off Devil Child babysitting to be able to go?
2. Will Sean be there ALONE – OR WITH LEAH?
3. Given that Leah will be there if she's going to promote them, whether she's WITH Sean or not . . . and given our, shall we call it, ambiguous situation, do I go alone or drag someone along for the ride?
4. Josh is a prize wally (he is!) but he's hot to look at, a professional photographer, cool dancer and MIGHT be persuaded to be my mate date (ha ha) so I don't look unloved.
5. But then am I shooting myself in the foot by dragging Josh along and so stymying any attempts by Sean to seduce me with his wild dance-floor moves? (Make me laugh more like – he's a great musician but his dancing's enough to make you cringe!)

Dilemma, dilemma, dilemma, dilemma, dilemma . . .

4 June

Boil the water. Cook the pasta. Grate the cheese. Keep the child away from the hob, from hot water, from hot pans. Keep the child entertained while you do this. Put the child safely on a chair. Concentrate on boiling pans on hob while child shrieks with joy as he covers himself in contents of bag of flour used for white sauce, or béchamel, whatever you like to call the basis of something you melt cheese into to make macaroni cheese for child's supper.

All this while Dad's in the house and could be keeping an eye on SOMETHING!

But no. Dad's doing important work.

Er, hello?? My work? My A levels clearly don't count as worth taking time over.

I'm not surprised SMAW says they have to put extra concealer under her eyes for photographs. And I've only done this for like three hours. Where's the chocolate? Not for him, for ME!

It's mind-numbing stuff. I mean, how am I supposed to decide whether to invite Josh to Sean and Mikey's party when I'm concentrating so hard on a child not burning himself that he manages to turn himself into a flour-covered ghost without my noticing until it's too late?

Josh is a slimeball.

Rebecca really fancies him.

They're friends.

These are three very good reasons to have nothing to do with the boy.

So I shan't. Have anything to do with him.

But what if I turn up at the party and Jill goes off with, say, Scratch? And if she's off with Scratch, and Sean's off with Leah, and Mikey's, like, much too focused on the music to have eyes for anyone but his sounds and their systems, I shall be left standing alone in a corner.

Besides: it would be cool, maybe, to see if turning up

with Josh got a reaction out of Sean. Wouldn't it?

But I can imagine the worst-case scenario of all. I decide to invite Josh. I invite Josh. Rebecca sees me do it and laughs when he knocks me back.

I'll have to text him . . . Email him . . .? Text . . .?

Help!

5 June

A way out . . .

Freedom!

If only I weren't so competitive!

Alice called me and Rebecca into her office today and told us she only has budget for one of us, and whoever proves most valuable will keep their job. Quick as a flash Rebecca says she'll get Alice a skinny blah blah latte and I find I'm running to beat her to the lift and I even skip the lift and skid down the stairs to get to the coffee shop first. Just because I can't bear to see Rebecca succeed. Pathetic! Imagine the hours I could have free. Hey, maybe I could make some more friends in that time so I have more than just Sean to get obsessed about. Maybe I'd have a life!

But, no. I joined in the game. Alice pressed those buttons. How can she make me do that? It was my chance to escape and I blew it.

And in the same spirit of all's fair in love and war, I'm not going down without a fight where Sean's concerned. The question, still, is whether I invite Josh.

Tom the counsellor and I had a real 'but if he knows

you know he knows you know' kind of conversation that got me strictly nowhere. He's so . . . correct about everything, Tom. I KNOW I don't always have to be in a relationship to justify my existence. I know I don't need defining by how attractive other people see me. But I'd like, for ONCE, not to be the single girl standing in the corner on my own. Or, rather, I'd like to be the one to CHOOSE whether I'm in the relationship or not. I want to be in charge of my love destiny, not at the mercy of other people's flights of romantic fancy.

6 June

It's all about manipulation, isn't it? Everything. Relationships, work, success, failure . . . it's all about how good you are at twisting things to suit you.

Well, listen here, turns out I'm about the worst manipulator the world has ever seen. I've got soooooooooo-ooooooo much to learn in this area I should go on a course!

I invited Josh to Sean and Mikey's party and yaaaaaaaaaaaaaay!

1. Rebecca didn't find out and
2. he said yes.

So at least I didn't have to turn up on my own! Actually, that was really worth inviting him for. If only the evening could have stopped there!

So, we make an OK entrance to the party. I have to

hold his hand cos the gaff's quite crowded and I don't want to lose him when he's my guest and I have to show him around a bit, don't I?

And Jill sees us. And Mikey sees us.

And Sean's there with Leah and they're holding hands (what is she doing with him?). So I drag Josh on to the dance floor and I dance like it was Jo and me in Stockport having the time of our lives. Never mind Josh dancing. Never mind how he was dancing. I wasn't out to impress him. And Sean and Leah had their heads together over the decks and he wasn't taking any notice of me. So I danced closer to Josh. And I manoeuvred us so we were dancing right in front of the decks so that we were directly in Sean's line of vision.

And STILL Sean took no notice.

And so, because I didn't care about Josh at all, and because I was desperate, I took Josh's face in my hands and I kissed him.

WHAT??????????????!!!!!!!!!!!!!!!

'Dear Jo,' I wrote. 'Cool party in a Shoreditch warehouse last night.'

Not such a cool Sofia, though.

What was I thinking of, copping off with Josh???????????????????

Am I going to work today?

Not in a million years.

I'm wagging it. School, work, everything. I can't do all this and not have time to digest it. I can't. Tom would agree with me. He WOULD!

9 June

It's horrible. Josh thinks I'm into him. I'm sooooooooooooo
not! I mean, I know he's seriously cute to look at and all
that but he's a bad boy, only interested in himself, and
when I got to work he was like edging me into the
stationery cupboard like we were going to be at it all day.

I had to tell him.

I said I was overexcited. It was the music. Whatever.
But I didn't mean to kiss him and he's got to get over it.

Hangdog? He suddenly looked like a shark that missed
its prey. Well, that and kind of like I'd kicked him in the
kidneys at the same time. It's a powerful business letting
people down. I don't like it. But at the same time . . . it
kind of gives me a kick – the kind of kick I don't like.
Too much of this and I'll turn into someone I don't want
to be.

If only Sean hadn't been so into Leah.

If only Leah didn't exist.

I mean, Sean might be being nice to Leah because of
the record deal.

Like he might have been being nice to me to get me
to give the demo to the A & R man.

I don't know. This is all waaaaaaaaaaaaaaaay too
complicated for me.

I would have let Josh down more gently but he was so
insistent. And we were at work. And I'm having a compe-
tition, remember, with Rebecca, to see who gets to keep
this job. I CAN'T let her win. Even if I can persuade my
dad to let me chuck the job AFTERWARDS because of

exams or something I've got to prove to Rebecca that she's not just to take for granted that she's always the best at everything . . .

I saw Sean and Jill at the coffee shop. Looks like the record deal's on. I'm pleased for them. For him. He's acting totally normal around me now. Like nothing ever happened or might have happened between us. I've obviously been reading waaaaaay too much into everything.

Like, I'm not saying I'm not glad I gave Josh the brush-off. But I'm seriously glad I didn't go to that party alone and declare my feelings to Sean or anything stupid like that. Sean clearly feels nothing but good mates' feelings for me. And I've got to get over that. But like Tom says, I could seriously do with some closure on this issue. Did I imagine everything between us? I mean, did he come on to me at that mate date at the cinema? Have I made, like, EVERYTHING up since then? We did kiss. He DID kiss me back at The Script. But then he gave ME the brush-off. Maybe I have just, like, a seriously overrated opinion of myself. Maybe I never stood a chance with him.

Well, here I am then. Another evening in the thrilling life and adventures of Sofia Taylor. Dylan sleeps peacefully after an astonishingly healthy supper of cheesy broccoli pasta and organic apple juice prepared entirely by his devoted half-sister (me!) – no chocolate in sight! Then only twenty minutes of the *Balamory* DVD, cuddling up with said devoted sister and then straight to bed with clean teeth and brushed hair and tucked up nicely with his teddy. I can't remember its name. Possibly something like Biggly Bear. Oh well, he's only two. There's a limit to how original a two-year-old can be when naming his nearest and dearest. He calls SMAW Pooh Pooh and we both think that's hysterical.

So it's almost ten o'clock and good girl Sofia's off to bed now with *The Mayor of Casterbridge* for company and A-level revision notes to cram into her tiny little brain. My, the excitement!

10 June

My life's shrinking. Only weeks . . . DAYS . . . ago I was bezzy mates with the hot new band of the moment. They asked me to do them the great favour of getting them noticed by the A & R man at Sony. I did. My efforts paid off. They're now about to be signed by Sony. And where am I?

I wrote things in this very book about things going round coming round, all good turns deserving another, etc.

Well, thanks to SMAW's re-launch as some kind of Liz Hurley mega model, I'm literally left holding the baby. Arghhhh. But I've found a way in which I can make the madness end.

There was a message on the machine about her needing to go back for a meeting. At FIVE O'CLOCK ON THURSDAY. You know what I'D like to be doing at five o'clock on Thursday? ANYTHING but aeroplane wheeeeeeeing spoonfuls of mush into Devil Child's mouth.

So I deleted the message.

I wrote it down.

I've got it. So if I lose my nerve . . .

But why should I tell her?

She LOVES Devil Child.

She wants to be his full-time mum.

My dad makes a good enough living for all of us.

None of us need the stress of her working again. LEAST of all me!

WHATEVER!

11 June

I'm just so KIPPERED all the time. I can barely function let alone contribute to twenty-first-century society. You know how it is when you get so tired you just feel like crying?

I went to work today because I have to or I'll lose that high-paying, high-status, serious-learning-curve (!*!*!*!) job at *Wicked*, and all day I felt light-headed with exhaustion. There was nothing to DO – as usual. So, rather than sit competing with Rebecca over who could sit up straightest, who could have the tidiest desk, who could get the most coffees fastest, I just went to indulge my malaise on the back stairs. Sometimes that's a really good place to be. They're kind of neutral, the back stairs of an office. It's like taking five in limbo land. Restful.

So I was just sitting there wondering if ever a day would

come when I didn't feel I was wasting my life away when Josh came to find me.

You know, he can be surprising, that boy.

He seemed really concerned. I told him about Devil Child and SMAW working and how kippered I am all the time and how I just don't think I can cope with the stress. It's not that what I have to do is particularly DIFFICULT: it's just that it's this never-ending list of chores and I never feel I'm catching up with myself. Work, and Devil Child, they're just distractions from what I'm supposed to be doing; they're slowing me down.

And he was so nice. Said he'd help me out where he can at *Wicked*. Said I'd helped him out before . . . Have I? Certainly not recently. But he was cool about that. So much less intense and complicated than Sean's being right now. Just, like, straight and normal and no atmospherics or anything. I might have SERIOUSLY misjudged the guy. Maybe he has this, like, veneer of not very cool selfishness but now, when he sees the *!*! hitting the fan in my life, all that pretence disappears and he's just unexpectedly kind.

Luckily, Alice caught us and accused us of flirting, which we were soooooooooo not, and it kind of de-intensified the moment – or I might have seriously cried on the boy's shoulder. How weird would that have been?

12 June

OK. So what goes around comes around? Maybe. Maybe it will. I've got to give things a chance.

If unexpected kindness comes from surprising quarters maybe THAT'S the recompense for being a good girl elsewhere.

Maybe it's not direct give and take. Maybe it's just how you feel. Maybe if you're receptive to the good stuff then you find it. And maybe being straight and honest helps keep you less wound up and therefore more receptive to the good stuff. Like personal feng shui. Yin and yang. Balance in all things.

Whatever.

I told SMAW about the message from her agent for the Boden shoot. Luckily I told her so late she had no time to give me a serious rollocking but just had to rush out of the house trusting me with Devil Child and the baking cupboard wide open to his destructive enthusiasms.

And it wasn't ALL bad. You know, the shoot didn't take forever. She was back by seven thirty. I went to see Sean and Mikey rehearsing in the studio. Jill's so made up about the whole thing. She's a good person. She's just, like, happy for them. She's not looking for any comeback for herself.

Jill kissed Scratch.

I TOLD you!

She couldn't stay the lonely ice princess forever and ever, goodly slaving over her economics homework with her law degree in view.

I'm glad for her.

*

I feel strangely Zen since that conversation with Josh. He really took me by surprise. There was clarity in his face, an honesty. For the first time since I've known him he wasn't after something. And it was a relief to have a conversation with a boy that wasn't full of anxiety about the things said and unsaid, what either person meant, who was hiding what. He was just nice to me, that's all.

I feel like a cloud's lifted, thanks to him.

I feel like it's all right to be on my own.

Maybe, though, I should chuck the idea of world domination, and take up philosophy instead?

You know when something absolutely perfect happens, you almost want to stop breathing for fear the noise of the oxygen going in and out will somehow blur the memory. I can't decide whether I should write all this down NOW in case of forgetting or whether the action of writing it will tarnish it somehow, so that I won't be able to find the words to say how perfect it was.

But I am writing already. And when the paper runs out, which it will in a minute, the pen's going to go all over the room and up over the ceiling before I manage to tell it all.

So, Sean texted me: 'Meet me in the park?'

I had to make myself calm.

I wore flip-flops and cut-off jeans shorts and my red-and-white-checked gingham cowgirl shirt and a waistcoat and some long, jangly, red plastic beads. No hat. Hair just down. Tiny bit of perfume on my wrists then rubbed behind my ears.

I found him sitting on the steps of the bandstand. He really is like a Labrador. I saw him before he saw me, and it was as if he could sense me coming. Suddenly his head's up and he's looking about him and then he's on his feet with a smile as wide as Waterloo Bridge.

'Hey,' he says.

And he reaches out and takes my hand and we walk along, like that, not speaking. I'd made a pact with myself on the way. I wasn't allowed to speak, to interrupt, to gabble on about nothing just to fill the silence. I was only going to be allowed to say something if it was worth saying.

And so we walked like that.

And it was one of those grey-blue afternoons when the rain's washed everything clean and the sun's just warming everything so that the grass smells delicious.

There was an ice-cream van and he bought us a double 99 flake and we shared it. No spoons. Just shared the ice cream. And he got some down his T-shirt and all over his chin and we laughed in relief because everything was all right and there were no more hang-ups between us.

And when we got back to the bandstand there was a bunch of brass-band players setting up there so we got tickets and everything. And while the band played the theme to *Titanic* on trombones and tubas we lay on the grass and still barely said anything.

I didn't ask about Leah.

He didn't tell.

But I know from the way he looked at me that Leah's just a promoter. He has to be nice to her. She's work. And I hope my eyes told him that Josh is just a guy I work with too. But I didn't dare open my mouth for fear of ruining the moment.

And long after the band had gone and the deckchair attendant had stacked them all beneath a great tarpaulin under a tree we finally got up, all creaky from lying on the damp grass.

And he walked me home, holding my hand and swinging my arm all the time.

And my dad must have liked him because he left us to say goodbye to each other in private on the doorstep: it was like being in a film. And then he took my face in his hands to kiss me.

And now I'm up here in my room, sailing away to fantasyland.

Maybe I will take up philosophy. But I think Sean and I have got a load of living to do first.

They're having a party tonight and the band are playing.

I'm so going to make something incredible to wear.

There's a skirt I could turn into a dress. And I've been customizing my baseball boots with sequins . . .